MW00533168

NO WAY OUT

BALLARAT CHARTER **LILA ROSE**

No Way Out Copyright © 2015 by Lila Rose

Hawks MC: Ballarat Charter: Book 4

Cover Image: Eric Battershell
Editing: Hot Tree Editing
Interior Design: Rogena Mitchell-Jones

All rights reserved. No part of this eBook or book may be used or reproduced in any written, electronic, recording, or photocopying without the permission from the author as allowed under the terms and conditions under which it was purchased or as strictly permitted by applicable copyright law. Any unauthorized distribution, circulation or use of this text may be a direct infringement of the author's rights, and those responsible may be liable in law accordingly. Thank you for respecting the work of this author.

No Way Out is a work of fiction. All names, characters, events and places found in this book are either from the author's imagination or used fictitiously. Any similarity to actual events, locations, organizations, or persons live or dead is entirely coincidental and not intended by the author.

Second Edition 2019
ISBN: 978-0648483502

*To my sweet, smart, beautiful niece, Casey Ford.
Love you heaps, girl. I'm so proud with what you have already
accomplished in life. Love the times you come and stay with us,
and our usual ritual of watching scary movies... though
sometimes, I could do without that.*

CHAPTER ONE

STOKE

*A*nother brother laid in the ground. I fucking hated this shit. Tank passed a week earlier, and we—his biker brethren—were learning, while sitting in the funeral home, that Tank had a lot of secrets.

One such secret, got him killed.

Another secret shocked the fuck outta all of us.

That secret sat up at the front of the church, as the funeral director droned on and on about God, Tank and his life.

Tank was one man in the club who I didn't get along with. Still, he was a brother, and I wanted to show my respect for that, which was why I was there.

It was no secret that Tank was shifty, rude, and a bastard to women. But still, he always had our backs, no matter the situation. He loved to party hard, fuck harder and live life on the edge.

Which was how he got himself killed.

Talon knew more about Tank. He was a friend of Tank's, yet, he still didn't know everything there was to know. It was obvious no one in our club did.

Or else someone would have known the fucker was married, and that he was leaving behind two teenage children.

The service finished and we all moved outside. I stood in a group with Talon, Wildcat, Griz, Deanna, Killer, Chatter, Blue and his woman, of a year, Clary.

"Did anyone know about her?" Blue asked.

A negative note was shared among us.

Looking over Griz's shoulder, my eyes landed on her. Fuck, she was gorgeous. No, I didn't know her at all, but hell, my body wanted to know her in more ways than one.

What a dick move. Thinking of fucking her just as she has put her husband to rest.

Not my fault, she's stunning.

Licking my bottom lip, my eyes travelled over her body where she stood near the doors to the funeral home, as if she was waiting for someone. Her long, light brown hair shone in the late sun's rays. Her curvy body called for my hands. Her green eyes were red rimmed, but I saw no tears. Since I watched her throughout the service, I noticed only her children cried quietly at her side. Her body gave no indication that she had cried at all.

Maybe she was fighting it. Maybe she'd break when others weren't around.

Though, for some reason, I had an inkling that wasn't the case.

"Someone needs to bring her into the fold," Wildcat declared.

"Kitten," Talon started.

"No Honey, look at her. She's standing there protecting her kids, but no one, and I mean no one, has approached or spoken to her. So, in other words, no one has her back."

Talon rubbed a hand down his face and sighed. "Fuck. Fine. Go do your shit." With that, she beamed, and Wildcat and her posse of pussies started for Tank's misses.

We all watched on, and I was sure we all noticed when Tank's lady saw the women approaching, because her whole body stiffened. Her walls were coming up. I couldn't help but wonder why.

Zara held out her hand. Tank's woman looked down at it and said something, bringing her kids closer to her body. Kids who looked to be around about thirteen and sixteen if I had to hazard a guess, the thirteen-year-old a boy and the sixteen-year-old a girl. Both were glaring up at Wildcat and her posse.

She shook her head at whatever Zara said and Deanna stepped forward. I cringed. Hell Mouth was never one to go in smooth, or soft. From the woman's wide eyes, Hell Mouth had just fucked up. Chatter quickly stepped forward saying something, which went on for a while. Again, she shook her head and said something back. That was when her eyes looked over Zara shoulder/head, landing on our group.

The women turned toward us. Clary was the first to turn

3

back to the woman and say something, causing her to smile slightly, but again, she shook her head.

They were bombing out big time.

It was then the funeral director came out, the widow turned her and her kids away from the pussy posse, and started talking to him.

Wildcat, with a worried look upon her usually smiling face, turned around and started walking back toward us. In fact, all the women looked as though they were sad or worried.

As soon as they reached us, I asked, "What the fuck just went down?"

After boss man folded Wildcat into his arms, she said, "She doesn't want anything to do with us."

"How's that, kitten?"

"She's saying she'd just rather be left alone. Not that she doesn't appreciate us wanting to lend her a helping hand, but she's fine with her life as is. I get a feeling she doesn't like bikers."

A thought came to me.

"It's time for reinforcements," I said. Talon looked to me, and I added, "Call him. Wildcat, keep an eye on her. If she makes a move to leave, stall…"

"Malinda," Ivy supplied.

With a chin lift, I added, "Stall Malinda until he gets here." It wasn't right the woman was on her own after such a hard situation.

"Right." She nodded. Her and her posse walked closer toward Malinda.

Fucking stunning name. Malinda.

"Jesus, are you sure?" Blue asked.

"He's good at getting in. If anyone can crawl past her walls, it's him."

They all nodded. Talon lifted his phone, pushed a button and put it to his ear. After a second, he spoke into it. "We have a situation. We need you here. Yes, right, okay. Fuck, serious? Yeah. Fine." Talon hung up and groaned. "He'll be here soon."

While we waited, we watched. Thankfully, the funeral director kept Malinda involved in a conversation until we spotted our reinforcement jogging toward us.

"Hey, my lovin' bunch of men. You call and I'm here. What do you need from me besides my body?" Julian asked as he stopped beside Talon.

We all sighed. Julian was the equivalent of an over-excited puppy, one that you wished would just grow the fuck up and stop being annoying. The only problem with that was Julian was never going to grow up. Still, he was useful, and in tense moments, he knew how to relax women. I hated to fucking say it, and there was no way in hell I would ever tell him, but at times like these he was good to have around.

Griz filled him in on the situation. By the end, Julian gripped his chest and a sob tore through him.

"Christ, here we go," Killer mumbled. I chuckled beside him.

"Oh, my God. It warms my gay heart that you all wanted me here to help. Do you think I could patch in the club now, become a member?"

"Julian," Talon growled.

"I was kidding." He smiled and looked over to Malinda. "That beautiful, poor woman. Don't worry about a thing. This gay mama bear will take care of her. Though, we'll need to talk about a payment."

"Fuck no! I already agreed you can take the women out on a girls' night, which will no fuckin' doubt end in trouble. Now, you do this or I'll tell Matthew about you offering free butt massages to my brothers."

Julian glared at Talon. "You are a cruel man, Thor. But alas, my boy-toy already knows about that."

"Do you think he wants a reminder?" Talon smirked.

"No," Julian snapped. "You know it took him a month to get over it." With that, he spun on his heels and trotted over to Malinda and the funeral director. There, he interrupted and introduced himself. The funeral director soon took off, maybe finding Julian a little too much. From then, we watched as Julian flamboyantly worked his magic and had, within seconds, the kids laughing and Malinda smiling.

Now that was a fucking glorious sight to see.

"Women are fucking powerless against him," Griz grumbled.

"Why do they Goddamn love him?" Killer asked.

"Because he brings sunshine into our lives," Clary offered as the women walked up to us. Each man secured their women within their arms.

I did not want any of that shit.

Sex. That was all I cared about.

I'd been stung once, with Helen, Chatter's friend. She was down with getting it on with me, but then she realised a biker man wasn't for her. Instead, she went for some uppity college dude, which I didn't know until I found them in bed together. After that, she turned a cold shoulder on me, and since then, hasn't been in Chatter's life as much.

Love and emotional shit was not worth the fucking trouble.

Sticking to just random fuck partners was better.

Then no one got hurt.

Even though I was watching Malinda and I had a need to look out for her, it was all for one reason. I wanted to fuck her.

At least that was what I told myself.

However, from the stormy look, not only from her, but her kids, when they glanced in my direction, it was going to be a hard hunt to partake.

I smiled my megawatt smile and she actually cringed.

Well, fuck!

I then felt like a prick once again because I was trying to crack onto her at her fucking husband's funeral.

Yeah, not my best bloody move.

She wasn't going to be worth it, not with kids in tow anyway. I'd never fucked a woman who had kids, so why did I want to start now?

I wasn't.

Forget about her and her goddamn lips that already looked swollen as if she'd been kissed thoroughly.

Forget about her hand on Julian's arm as she smiled shyly up at him. I wanted to rip Julian's arm right off his fucking body for letting her have her hand on him, when it should be on me.

Christ. Fuck that shit.

I needed to get out of there, find some dumb bitch to take my hard cock. It had been pulsating the moment I laid eyes on Malinda.

Just as I was about to say a goodbye, I spotted Julian trotting our way as Malinda led her kids in the other direction.

A smiling Julian stopped beside Griz and announced, "How good am I? Anyone who wants to bow down and kiss my feet may."

Hell Mouth snorted. "No thanks, but you can tell us what went down."

"Malinda, her son, Josh, and her daughter, Nary, are coming to the barbeque tomorrow to celebrate the life of her husband, Tank, at the compound."

"What barbeque?" Wildcat asked.

Julian grinned wide. "The one you now have to organise so we can bring the introvert Malinda and her monsters into our fold. She needs this. Her children need this because I have a feeling they are a handful, and Malinda is at her wit's end. With her hubby now gone, she'll need all the help we can give her."

"You're amazing." Clary giggled.

"Oh, buttercup, thank you. And I think as my reward, I should get a kiss on the cheek from every biker in the club." He tapped his cheek and tilted his head toward Griz.

"No fucking way," Griz growled.

"All right, my women," Zara called. "In light of my hubby losing a brother, and in light of taking more into our posse, it's time to get things organised for this get together tomorrow. Who's with me?" She put her hand in the middle of our circle. Ivy was the first to lay hers on top, then Julian, then Clary and they all turned to look at Hell Mouth.

"Jesus fucking Christ, all right." She lay her hand on top. They then all took off after laying some love on their partners.

Once they were out of earshot, Talon turned to us. "Tonight, we meet. We need to figure out all the shit that Tank was involved in. Figure out if his death is cause for us to retaliate, and we need to figure the fuck out if whatever he did, will bring crap to Malinda's doorstep."

With a chin lift, we parted. There was no way I was missing that meet.

CHAPTER TWO

MALINDA

*M*y husband had died. I should be grieving but I wasn't. I should be upset; yet, I wasn't, even though I had just buried him.

Why?

I knew the answer. It was hard to take, to understand, and some people wouldn't. They'd see me as some cold-hearted bitch. I wasn't. At least I didn't think I was.

Cry dammit.

Nope, nothing.

Feel… but I didn't. I felt nothing.

I pinched myself hard. *There we go.* My eyes started to water.

Only to stop.

Christ.

Terry May, also known as Tank, and I were married when we were both eighteen, when I first become pregnant with our daughter, Nary. In the beginning our marriage was blissful. He treated me as if I was the most precious person in his life. He worked hard, but when he came home, he had time for both Nary and myself. Two years later, Josh came into our lives; again, things were going along great. Yes, we had our little fights, but nothing we both couldn't handle or work through.

It wasn't long after Josh was born when Tank told me he was leaving his old biker club and joining a new one, the Hawks. He thought highly of them, and I wasn't one to argue over a matter like that, not when he was happy to be a part of a club in the first place.

Things changed from there. It was little things to start with. He'd come home drunk, and when Josh would wake from the noise Tank was making, he would become angry, yell and then climb into bed fully-clothed only to pass out. The following day, he wouldn't rise until very late. He be cranky and want to leave the house as soon as he could. I asked him many times what was going on, but he wouldn't tell me. He told me nothing, or that it wasn't any of my business.

A week before my twenty-first birthday, he came home with his brother, Oscar. He walked through the front door and ordered me to take the children out for the day. His brother had always freaked me out; I never liked the way his eyes sought me out. The gleam in them told me he wanted to do bad things, but I was protected, *just*, because I was his brother's wife.

I didn't know what went down that day. They both seemed edgy, yet excited about something. Still, I listened and left with the children.

It was one week later.

One week later, on my twenty-first birthday, I fell out of love with my husband.

Even though he was acting strangely, even though he was moody day after day, I never, not ever, thought my heart could shatter in all but a moment.

And my love for him would die.

But it did.

It did because the night of my twenty-first birthday, I had the children minded by our neighbour, Mrs Cliff. She was a dear old soul and would do anything for a person. So the children went there for the night. I ran around the house in a tizzy, wanting to make everything perfect, because even though it was my birthday, I wanted it special for us. We hadn't bedded one another for at least a month, and I was more than ready.

I dressed in a garter, panties and a sexy hot-pink corset. I remember smiling to myself that night. I was giddy with excitement and thrilled as I thought of what the night would hold.

I was going to get a bit, and my lady bits were crying with glee. "Bow-Chica-Wow-Wow" kept playing over and over in my head.

Until, that was, he came through the front door drunk.

Standing just inside the front door after hearing the loud pipes of his Harley coming down the street, the smile soon flew from my mouth once I saw him staggering.

He took one look at me through hazy eyes and slurred with a vicious voice, "Who in the fuck are you dressed up for?" He took another step in and slammed the door closed. "You expecting your lover to come here?"

"What? No," I cried, annoyed he could even think that. I had only ever been with one man and that man was swaying slightly in front of me.

"Bullshit," he spat. He advanced toward me with hatred in his eyes, and for the first time, I backed away from my husband. "You look like a stupid, fat slut."

"Tank, baby, I did this for you," I said, pain lacing my voice. His words gutted me.

"Well, I don't like my wife looking like the whores I fuck at the club."

A tear ripped through my heart.

"Take it off, *now!*" he bellowed.

I didn't even get a chance to move. He was on me in seconds and tore the clothes roughly from my body. I whimpered and cried as he hands groped hard, pulling all the clothes away.

"Fuck," he hissed. "Even having you naked isn't an improvement. Why in the hell did I marry such an ugly bird?"

My heart cracked open wider from his cruel words.

"Go and put your stupid fucking nightie on. Then I may fuck you. That's if I can even get it up."

"Please don't talk to me like this," I pleaded.

He got close, gripped my jaw in a tight squeeze and barked in my face, "I will talk to you how I want. I will do with you what I like. It's time you learned how to act. You're just the bitch I come home to, who keeps my house clean and takes care of my kids."

"No," I whispered to the ground. I closed my eyes and knew I couldn't take it. I shouldn't take it. With my left hand, I reached up, took hold of his wrist and pushed it from my face. I looked up, glared into his eyes and yelled, "No. You will not do this to me. To us. This isn't you, Tank."

He laughed without humour and slapped me across the face. "Learn your place, bitch. Never talk to me like that again and do as you're fucking told." With that, he shoved me to the ground and repeatedly planted his foot into my stomach, until I was spitting blood from my mouth. He leaned over and hit me twice more in the face. From there, he turned and walked toward the hall where our bedroom lay. Over his shoulder, he said, "Don't bother coming to bed. I don't want you in it. You deserve to sleep on the floor like the dog you are."

I couldn't have moved even if I tried.

That night I lay on the living room floor crying in agonising pain until I passed out.

But before I drifted into unconsciousness, I knew my heart bled more than what flowed from my mouth.

My heart was torn wide open, and from it, my love for the man I married poured out.

It flowed out leaving nothing but agony behind.

That was the day I fell out of love.

Some may think I was crazy to have stayed with him. Some would even understand why I did.

I had my own reasons.

Still, I never really understood them myself.

If I left, I would have lost so much: the house, the money, the safety.

They were ridiculous excuses.

The most ridiculous one was that I didn't want to start over. I didn't want to have to find another man, because what happened if I did and he was worse than Tank?

And really, I was a mother of two children... who would have wanted me?

So I stayed.

I stayed in hope that things would get better. That he would be the husband I knew he could be, had been. That he'd be the father that he could be and had been when Nary was born.

But he didn't. He no longer was.

What also had me staying was because the next morning, when Tank came from the bedroom and spotted me naked, bruised and bloody on the floor, he swore and ran to me.

"Baby, fuck, baby. What happened? Who did this to you?"

He didn't remember.

When I whispered the words, "You." I saw the pain in his eyes. I saw them widen in shock, regret filled him as everything he did came crashing into his mind.

Tears pooled in his eyes. He reached out to my face only to pull back and wince. "Fuck. Christ!" he yelled into the room. He got up from the floor dressed in only boxers and ran down the hall. He came back with a sheet and laid it over my cold body. "Please... fuck, baby. I didn't mean it. I never meant anything I said or did. I couldn't control it. I couldn't stop myself. I was high, baby."

"Hospital," I managed to gasp out.

"Right, of course, fuck."

He got me to the hospital; I had two broken ribs, a fractured cheekbone, and bruises all over. Of course, they questioned how it happened. I used what most women would use in that type of situation—I had fallen down some stairs. Without any witnesses, they couldn't do anything but patch me up and release me.

Tank then went next-door and asked Mrs Cliff to have the children again. He told her I had fallen and hurt myself, and that he needed to take care of me. She did, because there wasn't much Mrs Cliff wouldn't do. She may have been a bit eccentric, but she was sweet and had a safe place for the children to stay.

After that day, Tank was different once again. He wasn't his normal self, like he was when we met. He wasn't that mean, cranky man either. Instead, he was quiet, cold and lifeless. I knew he regretted what he had done to me. Even though he didn't say it, I saw the pain in his eyes. But I couldn't come to forgive him, so I couldn't reassure him.

We lived with each other and that was all.

Even though we slept in the same bed, long gone were the light caresses and touches of love. He slept on his side and me on mine.

We talked calmly to one another, but there were no smiles, no laughter and no love any longer between the two of us.

It had been like that until the day he died.

His body was discovered in bushland. A gunshot wound to the chest, which went straight through his heart.

Someone had meant to kill him. I knew this; the police knew this, and I was sure his biker brothers knew this.

What we didn't know was why.

Hope.

That was all I could do, hope that whatever and whoever had caused his death, didn't find its way back to me, to the house and my children.

"Mum?"

Glancing over my shoulder from the front window, to Nary, my sixteen-year-old daughter, I smiled. She looked so much like me. Standing in the kitchen doorway, she had her mobile to her ear.

"Yes, honey?" I smiled.

Should I be smiling? I wasn't sure. I was going crazy with thoughts of how I should act. What would a normal woman do if she lost her husband? I screwed up my face, causing Nary to raise her eyebrows at me. Damn, I just looked weird, so I wiped my face clear and waited to see what she wanted.

"Can I go to Mitch's?"

Closing my eyes, I turned my head back to the window and took a deep breath. I knew the situation would need my full attention so I spun my whole body around. "No, honey. We just buried your dad. I think it's good to stay home, yeah?"

She rolled her eyes. "It's not like it's that big a' deal. He didn't really care about us. Why should we care about him?" said the girl who cried her eyes out in the church.

"Nary, please, just stay home tonight."

"Jesus Christ, Mum."

"Nary!" I yelled. "Watch your mouth." The little shit was getting an attitude, just like I had at her age. I knew how much of a terrible teen I was, so that thought left me cringing.

She glared at me. "Whatever." Then she spun around and said into the phone, "Sorry, Mitch, I have to stay home and pretend I cared about my loser father who treated us all like we were lepers." She snorted. "The warden will let me out tomorrow."

"No," I called. She stomped back into the living room. "We're going to see your father's friends."

"I'm not going," she whined.

She had to. I wanted both Nary and Josh close to me in case anything did arise after their father's death.

"You are, and I don't want to hear more about it. You either do this or no phone for a month," I said.

She gasped. "You wouldn't."

"I would, honey. You know this."

"Why are you being so mean after we buried Dad?"

Oh, God.

Did she not see how funny her saying that was? When only moments ago she said she didn't care.

I knew she did. She knew she did, and we both knew Josh did.

Tonight was for my children. We would reminisce on good times... even if they were few and far between.

CHAPTER THREE

MALINDA

*S*tanding out the front of a biker's compound on a warm sunny day was not my favourite thing to do. Even being there wasn't on my favourite one hundred things to do. Yet, there we were, and all I had to do was walk in there with my children and pretend everything was okay.

Instead, I wanted to pee myself.

Or throw up chunks.

However, I knew I could do this. I'd had many moments of acting, pretending everything was okay. People who hardly knew me bought the act easily.

Still, something told me these people, the bikers' women, would be able to see through my act and want to help with the problems that lay beneath my fake.

Another reason I wanted to pee myself.

"Mum," Josh whined. "Can we get this over and done with? I was playing an awesome game on the Xbox with Dave, I want to get back to it."

My brows drew together as I looked down at my boy. "How were you playing this game when Dave wasn't at our house?"

Nary snorted. "Jesus, Mum, how dumb are you?"

Glaring at my daughter, I warned, "You use that language toward me one more time, Nary, you will be grounded,"

Josh took hold of my wrist and explained, "It's wireless. We can join games over the internet."

"Oh," I said and looked back to the compound.

It wasn't what I expected a compound to look like. It was big, scary in a way, but clean, seemingly safe. To the side of it was a mechanics business.

Why couldn't I take that final step toward towards the entrance?

Because I was still scared. Hence, the peeing and chucking thoughts.

Tank had been a biker and he had warned me about other bikers. They were rough, loud and brutal. I had asked him why he joined. His explanation was because he felt he had a family in them when he didn't have one when he was growing up.

Even though he had been a biker, to start with, he was nothing like he explained bikers to be; until that was, he changed to this club.

Another reason I was apprehensive to enter.

I was worried I'd find something out and want to cut any mothertrucker who ended what had been a blissful marriage and changed it to hell on earth.

Though, what I couldn't understand was how could this biker club, the club that drove my husband to the mean man he had been, allowed the likes of Julian around?

It had been interesting meeting Zara, Deanna, Clary and Ivy. They tried to get me to warm to them, but having their men watching from a distance had my back up. I thought it was some trick for some stupid reason, so I didn't want to trust them. They had seemed nice enough... Deanna, I wasn't too sure of though; her potty mouth left a lot to be desired in front of my children. Even if I swore under my breath or in my head just as much.

So when Julian had come strolling on up, it became even more interesting. He'd made Josh and Nary laugh, even on a day that held misery, I was thankful for that. From the first second he was in our presence, I was comfortable around him while he talked about nonsense. Then he told me he was a part of the gang of bikers. I was shocked to say the least.

The question that played on my mind was if having Julian as a comfort blanket was going to be enough to walk into a biker's compound, when I swore black and blue that I would never step foot in one?

Nope, it wasn't.

I couldn't do it. If that made me a chicken, then so be it.

"Um... I think we should go," I started to say when someone from behind called out, "Hi." I turned around, as

21

did Josh and Nary to see a handsome man, about twenty-one or two, walk across the road.

"Hi," I said back cautiously.

He came to a stop beside us and smiled. "Are you Malinda?"

My eyes widened in surprise. "Yes." Was he a clairvoyant?

"I'm Mattie. My partner told me you were coming today. He's already in there."

Oh. "He?" I asked.

"Yeah." He grinned. "Julian, I believe you met him yesterday."

That time I smiled. "Yes, he, um, invited us here today."

"Great, then what are you doing out here?" he asked, shifting from one foot to another.

"I… ah, I—"

"They're a good group of people, Malinda."

I studied him. He was serious and I wanted to believe him. I did. But I was still a cautious person, beside the fact that I was freaking the fuck out on the inside.

"Hey." Mattie gave a chin lift to Nary and Josh.

"Sorry, this is Nary and Josh," I said.

"Nice to meet you both. Could I, um, have a word with your mum quickly?" Mattie asked. Both children looked at me. I gave a small nod and they stepped away. I rolled my eyes when they both took out their phones and started playing with them.

"Malinda." I looked back to Mattie. "I can't honestly know how you're feeling, but I give you my word no harm will come to you or your family from those people in there," He pointed to the compound. "My sister is married to their president. She's a smart woman. She wouldn't risk her own children's life. If you don't feel safe at any time, come and get me or Julian. Even any of the women, we will have your back." He smiled. "But I can tell you, the men in there, they're good guys. They don't deal in any bad things." He took a breath and ran a hand through his hair. He met my eyes with concern showing in their depths. With his voice low, he continued, "I'm so sorry for your loss, but I know, whatever your husband was involved in has nothing to do with this club. Talon runs a tight, clean ship. If he didn't, he would lose his wife, his brothers' wives and his family. He wouldn't want that." He reached out and took my hand. "You'll be safe in there. Your children will be safe. I know it will be hard to understand, but my Julian said from the look in your eyes yesterday, you didn't trust bikers, even though your husband was one. But the men in there are different from your husband. I'm sorry to say that, honey."

I nodded. It was so much to take in. He truly believed they were the good guys. I supposed there was only one way to find out for myself. I had to go into the lion's den to see for myself.

"He... my husband, he changed... he was a good man until he joined this club," I explained.

Mattie looked startled. "That doesn't make sense to me. I've known these men for two years, Malinda, and I know they're decent people who would do anything for those they care for. They would even lay their lives down for those they care for. Some even have. Thankfully, they survived. So

I'm sorry, but I can't see this club being the cause of how your husband changed."

Wow. They sounded amazing. They sounded like a good group of people to get to know. My stomach lurched. I fought it back, wishing Tank had shown us this when he had joined. But he didn't. He kept that part of his life separate and I didn't understand why.

"Okay," I whispered. "I have a feeling I can trust you and Julian, but if I see anything I don't like, for me or my children, then I'm leaving and I'm sorry, but I won't want anything to do with anyone involved in this club."

"I can understand that." He grinned.

He had faith. I could see it. I just wasn't sure I could believe it. I was about to find out.

Calling to Nary and Josh, I turned with Mattie to the compound and took a deep breath.

STOKE

Sitting out the back of the compound shooting the shit on a sunny afternoon was something I didn't mind doing. It sucked we'd lost a brother, but what was worse was what we learned in our meeting. Tank had been involved in some heavy shit, and Talon, no not just him, but all of us were fuckin' pissed a member of our brotherhood would even think to deal in coke behind our backs. Our club didn't stand for that shit. Our club was clean and safe. But he took it upon himself to be a shady cunt and deal in goddamn coke with some mean motherfuckers, that's what got him shot.

Talon had brothers scouting to see what else could be found out. To see if there was more Tank was conspiring with, and if he was, would that crap blow back on us, the club? Fuck, not only us, but Tank had a missus and kids. If the men who killed him didn't like the deal that went down, others who were close to Tank could have trouble coming their way.

Talon ordered protection for Malinda and her kids straight after he found out Tank's dealings. We all knew it was going to be one hell of a time, because she already showed that she didn't trust us.

She'd have to deal if she wanted to stay safe.

The back door opened up, I turned from talking to Killer and Dodge to see Mattie walk through. I was just about to turn back around, but the person who came through after Mattie had my full attention. Even though I sensed others walk out after her, my eyes stayed glued to her curves that swayed as she walked. Mattie led her to the women's group over in the corner under a large shady oak tree, protecting the little monsters from the warming sun.

Christ, she looked stunning, even though she only wore jeans and a tee. But those jeans hugged her arse nicely and that tee splayed tightly over her more-than-a-handful breasts.

Breasts I wouldn't mind slipping my dick between.

"Why don't you just go over there?" Killer asked.

I turned back to my brother and smirked. I took a pull of my beer and shook my head. "She ain't my type."

Dodge snorted. "Tell your eyes and tongue that; they seem to be hanging outta your head as soon as she walked in."

"Fuck off," I hissed. They both laughed, then we all turned back to watch the show. Julian was the first to stand. He hugged Malinda, and I swore under my breath. The introduction went around the group, even though she'd already met them the previous day. My eyes stalked her mouth as she spoke and introduced her kids. Wildcat said something and pointed to Josie who was talking with Cody and Maya to the side. Wildcat's parents were usually there, but they had to go do some other shit. They dropped Josie off to spend time with her sister and family. Malinda's kids soon slunk off toward Josie.

Malinda took a garden seat next to Ivy. Killer patted me on the back. "I'm goin' over, you comin'?"

"Sure," I said, not really paying attention. Dodge chuckled and walked off to the barbeque area where Talon and Blue were.

As we made our way over, Malinda sensed us coming. Turning, she looked and stiffened. Mattie, who was sitting on her other side, touched her arm. She looked to him and nodded.

"Oh, oh, oh," Ivy started and I braced, "Malinda, I'd like you to meet my man Fox. Though, everyone here calls him Killer. It's a thing the biker dudes do for each other, with the whole nickname thing, and then when a female joins the group. They get a name too. Like me, I'm Chatter. You can probably tell why. I talk a lot. Usually it's when I'm nervous...or when everyone is so quiet, like now, then again, it's easy for everyone to go quiet when I'm around. Really, I could probably talk enough for everyone. Anyway, as I was saying, I'm Chatter and Zara gets called Wildcat, and Deanna, you met her yesterday. She should be here soon. She's called Hell Mouth. I just bet you can guess why; sometimes her swearing's worse than the guys. Oh, my God," her eyes widened. "I just realised we haven't got a name for you, Clary. We must think on this."

"Woman," I sighed.

"Stoke, goodness, sorry. Malinda, this is Stoke." She leaned closer to Malinda and whispered, "His real name is Declan. Kickarse name I think. What about you? But not as kickarse as Fox." She beamed. Malinda simply nodded. She looked stunned, as we all were when we first met and really talked to Ivy. No one could understand how so many words could come out of her sweet mouth in such a short amount of time.

Malinda looked from Fox to myself. Fox gave her a chin lift. I went in for the kill and sent her a wide smile. Her brows drew down.

Zara soon took away Malinda's attention. "Malinda, how are you holding up?" She sent a small, concerned smile to Malinda as she bounced a wiggly Ruby on her knee. I looked to see Drake sitting on the rug where the chairs were surrounding, chewing on something that looked plain and boring.

I took a seat opposite her as Killer went and stood behind his woman's chair. He bent and whispered something in Ivy's ear, causing her to blush. Fuck, he was a lucky bastard. Ivy was amazing. So happy and carefree, but so fucking loyal. She was perfect for my brother, who was a brother in more ways than one. I never thought Killer would dig his way out of the darkness that surrounded him. But he did, and it was because of Ivy. For that alone, I would be forever grateful to that woman.

"I'm… um, okay." She bit her bottom lip as an indication she didn't want to talk about it, and I couldn't blame her. She was surrounded by people she didn't know.

"How old are your monsters, Lindy?" We all looked to Julian. He slid off his seat to sit on the rug with Drake. Drake grinned up at him as Julian pulled a funny face and made a noise from his mouth. Well, I sure hoped to fuck it came from his mouth.

"Are you talking to me?" Malinda asked.

"Yeah, sweetie. I'll christen you… until the men get to know you. Lindy, short for Malinda." He smiled and tickled Drake who giggled with glee.

"Oh." She licked her lips. I watched her tongue with interest. "Nary is sixteen and Josh is fourteen."

"So that makes them both in high school. Must be a handful." Zara smiled nicely.

Malinda nodded. "They both like trying me."

"Josie, my adopted sister, will be graduating at the end of the year. She's only been with us for two years, but it seems longer. They do seem to grow up too fast."

Malinda smiled sadly. "Yes, they do." I didn't like seeing that sad smile upon her gorgeous face. Thank fuck, it wasn't there for long.

The back door opened and out stepped Hell Mouth who then shouted, "I'm knocked up." Griz came out behind her, smiling like a proud man and holding Swan in his arms. She kicked free of her dad's hold, and once her feet were on the ground, she took off for Maya. Stepping closer to his woman, Griz slid one arm across Hell Mouth's chest; he brought her back against him as he said something to her. She laughed. "Sorry, my man, who is big and strong and mighty, knocked me up."

That was when the women went crazy. Some squealed, mostly Julian, but all made their way over to congratulate the happy couple. That was until Wildcat came back and tried to dump a squirming Ruby on my lap. I held my hands up and yelled, "Whoa, woman, what the hell are you doin'?" Despite my protest, she sat her down.

"Just hold her 'til I come back. Then you can congratulate them." Zara giggled and quickly took off.

"Wait," I yelled in a panic now. "What do I do?" I looked to Killer. Shrugging, he smirked his arse off. With wide eyes, I looked to the only person left, Malinda, scared as fuck. I didn't do children. "What do I do? Shit, help, it's moving!" I snapped as Ruby shifted around to look at me. "What does it need? Food? A drink? Hell, I can't feed you, little person. I don't have milk in me." My head rose slowly and I hissed, "Christ, what happens if it needs to poop? Zara?" I barked across the lawn.

"Man up, big boy," came from Wildcat.

That was when I heard a tinkle of laughter. My head snapped around to glare at Malinda as she covered her mouth with her hand and laughed behind it.

"This ain't funny, woman. Look at it. Hell, it's straining. It's doing it; I can tell. It's pooping because it knows I won't like it. Now, listen here, little one, keep that stuff inside you. Do. Not. Poop."

Doubled over, laughing her sexy arse off, I looked over at Malinda in disbelief. Killer was just as bad, chuckling at my expense, standing at her side.

"Brother, take it." I held Ruby out.

"Shit no," Killer answered around his laughter.

"Fuck, fuck, fuck," I chanted. "The other one is looking at me. No, no, stay there, little dude." Christ, Drake was crawling my way. I quickly stood from the chair, took two steps forward and planted Ruby in Malinda's lap.

She sobered her laughing enough to say to Ruby, "Did that mean man scare you?" She laughed again and added, "I think you scared him even more." I sat back in my chair and nodded. I was totally on board with that. Kids could be scary. My eyes met with emerald green ones when Malinda looked over at me. "They're not that scary." She smiled. "She may like it if you stopped calling her an it. What's her name?"

"Ruby," I said.

"You are a beautiful girl, little Ruby," she cooed down at her.

"You don't know what you're talking about!" We heard shouting. Everyone turned to look over at Cody in the face of Malinda's boy, Josh.

"Oh, no," Malinda uttered. She got up from her seat and with Ruby on her hip. She dashed over to her son, with Killer and me on her heels.

"It's obvious she isn't your real mum. Get over it," Josh yelled back in Cody's face.

"Josh," Malinda gasped.

"Cody?" Zara said as she came up beside Malinda. Malinda quickly passed Ruby to Wildcat as Zara told Mattie to go to Drake. I stood back a bit to see how it would play out.

"You need to shut your mouth. She is my mum and just because you're angry your stupid dad died doesn't mean you can say shit to me," Cody yelled.

"Cody Marcus," Zara snapped.

"What?" Cody growled. He caught himself and his tone toward Wildcat and stepped back from Josh. "He said you weren't my mum." Cody glared at Josh.

"Josh, why would you say such a thing?" Malinda asked.

Josh looked over his shoulder to his mum, shrugged and then said, "Everyone knows at school his real mum didn't want him."

They were in school together. Interesting. They looked about the same age. Maybe they were in the same grade.

Cody made a leap for Josh. Talon was there in a flash and grabbed his son. Malinda, with shoulders slumped, smacked her son in the back of the head. "Apologise right now."

"Mum," Josh whined.

"Now," she snapped, and fuck, it if that didn't turn me the hell on.

He mumbled, "Sorry."

"And *I'm* so sorry about this," Malinda uttered. "We better get going anyway." She took her son's arm in hand and started for the back door. Her daughter silently followed.

31

"Lindy," Julian called. "You don't have to go."

"No, I should," she stated, and looked to me, and then back to Julian.

What was that?

"I'll walk you out," Mattie offered.

Me? I stood there like a fuckin' pining fool.

I really needed to get laid.

After she was through the door, Talon turned to his son. "Fuckin' proud you wanted to stick up for yourself, but you don't let shit like that get to you. He's going through some crap at the moment and trying to find a way to let it out."

"I know, Dad." Cody sighed.

"Honey," Zara glared at her husband. "Watch your mouth." Talon's lips twitched. Ignoring it, Zara turned to Cody, "You also, young man. Now let's get you fed. Just like your father, maybe if I calm your beast inside with a good feed, you wouldn't have needed to yell." She took a step toward Cody and laid her hand on his cheek. "No matter what anyone says, I am your mum." With that, she kissed his cheek. Cody blushed and shrugged out of her hold embarrassed.

"I know," he said with an eye roll.

"Let's fuckin' eat," Talon called.

"Talon," Zara warned.

Family. Too much shit to deal with. I could handle it with just the brothers of the club, but not with any kids. That was something I knew I never wanted.

The back door opened and I turned to it... Christ almighty, I had hope in me that Malinda was back... even with her kids.

What. The. Fuck.

I just contradicted myself.

Instead, it was Helen, Ivy's old best mate and my ex —sort of.

It was definitely time for me to get the fuck outta there!

CHAPTER FOUR

MALINDA

"What in your right mind drove you to do that, Josh?" I asked on the drive home. Mattie had walked us out. He asked for my phone, and without thinking, because I was still shocked with what Josh had done, I'd given it to him. He fiddled with it and said he placed all his contacts in there, telling me that if I ever needed him, to call. I said a quiet thank you, never knowing people to be so kind without really knowing me. I was surprised he wanted to reach out to me even more.

"I don't know," Josh said quietly from the backseat.

"It was a dick move," Nary offered.

I turned my head to glare at her. "Nary," I warned and took a deep breath. "Josh, honey. You have to know why you said it. Please tell me."

Looking in the rear-view mirror, I caught his eye roll. But the look on his face told me he knew, and he was not only angry, but upset. "Maybe 'cause he was braggin' about how good his family is. Maybe it's 'cause we only just buried Dad yesterday and he was talking about how good *his* dad is, when I had a dad who didn't give a shit about us. I had a dad who showed us nothing but that we were a waste. I wanted him to hurt like I was. Happy now?" he yelled.

Oh, God.

My heart bled for my child.

Tears filled my eyes, but I blinked them away. I had to be strong for him, not just for Josh, Nary as well. "Honey," I uttered. "I'm sorry. I shouldn't have taken us there today. But, Josh, please believe me, your dad did love you. He may not have shown it, but he did. He was just going through a bad time"

"What, for freakin' fourteen years? Mum… don't. Don't stick up for him. Nary and I saw how he was. He didn't like us and he didn't like you."

"Baby, he did. He really did like you both."

Josh snorted. "Yeah, okay, Mum."

Damn it to hell. I should have left him. For *my* children's sake, I should have left him. Maybe then he would have been a better father. I sighed. He wouldn't have, but at least then I could have protected my children more.

I'd failed.

Failed as a mother because I was too scared.

It wasn't fair on them. I should have seen that. As a result, I'll regret it for the rest of my living life.

I wanted to slap my forehead and cry to the sky. I

wanted to crawl into a ball and yell that the world wasn't fair. My children didn't deserve what they felt and it was my fault.

As we pulled into the driveway, I turned in my seat and caught Nary and Josh's eyes. "I'm sorry. I'm so sorry you both feel this way. Most of all, I'm sorry I didn't protect you both from it. All I can tell you, all that I can hope is that you both find my love enough to keep this family going. Because I do love you both with all of my heart. I always will, no matter what you do. I hope you feel that love and know you both can come to me any time you need to. You can talk to me about anything, and I will try my best to support you in every way I can."

Nary's eyes softened, something I hadn't seen in a long time. Josh smiled at me shyly—that was also something that had been rare, I should have noticed both before.

"We know, Mum," Nary said. "I love you, too."

My bottom lip trembled. There was my beautiful girl.

"Yeah, uh, me too. That… I love you, too and I'm sorry about today."

Oh, dear. And there was my precious little boy.

I wiped the tears that had escaped away and smiled brightly. "Thank you, both of you." I clapped my hands together and announced, "Now, I think this evening calls for a good dose of comedy movies and pizza. What do you think?"

"Sounds great," Nary said. "I'll just go and call Mitch. Tell him I'm not coming over." I thanked the Lord above that Mitch was gay, or else there would be no way I would let my sixteen-year-old daughter near an eighteen-year-old boy.

"That'd be awesome, Mum, but make sure you get a real man's pizza, with all meat."

Nary and I both laughed.

IT WAS after we'd eaten our way through two large pizzas, and after we had watched *Let's be Cops*, there was a knock at the front door. I looked to the clock on the set-top box. It read seven pm. *Who's here at this time?* The children had just gone into the kitchen to make some chocolate sundaes, so I got up from the couch to answer it.

Only upon opening it, I tried to close it just as quickly.

But it was too late.

A black dress shoe was shoved inside and a weight leaned against the door pushing it back toward me. I stumbled back a few steps, and that was when Oscar, Terry's brother filled the door way, and he looked pissed.

"W-what are you doing here?" I stuttered while I prayed the children would stay in the kitchen without making a sound.

"Tell me where it is," he hissed. He took another step in and slammed the door closed.

"I-I don't know what you're talking about," I told him and moved further into the living room, so his back would be to the kitchen.

"I think you do. You just want to keep it all. My brother

said you were a stupid, selfish bitch. But I thought, such a pretty little woman wouldn't be like that."

Oh, God.

What had Terry been involved in with Oscar?

I didn't know what he was talking about...what he wanted. He looked as though he'd just come from work. He was dressed in a suit, one like he wore every day at his car dealership.

"Please, if you just tell me what you're after, I'll get it," I said, backing up another step until my body hit the wall next to the television.

He stomped right up to me as my heart went crazy, and laid his hand against my neck. "Where's the bag, Malinda?"

"What bag? I don't know what you're talking about."

"Such a pretty little neck you have." He placed pressure against my neck as he spoke. "Yes, a very pretty neck, I would hate to see it broken, Malinda."

My eyes widened and while he moved his head closer to breathe me in, something moved near the kitchen that caught my gaze. I glanced over Oscar's shoulder to see Nary on a phone. I tried to shake my head, but she just shook hers back. I mouthed, "Go." She shook her head again as tears fell onto her cheeks.

Leaning his face closer, his lips touched my ear, Oscar whispered, "I want that bag, Malinda. If I don't have it, I'll have your neck. If that doesn't scare you enough, I'll have your kids as well."

"No," I cried. No one threatened my children. I pulled back my fist, in the tight gap he allowed between our bodies, I punched him in the stomach. "You leave them alone," I screamed.

"Fuck," he roared and backhanded me so hard my body went sideways, hitting the TV cabinet and falling to the floor in front of it.

"Y-you need to leave," Nary said, stepping fully into the living room. "I called people. They're on their way. I called the police and they'll be here too."

"Nary, no," I cried.

Oscar started for her. She let out a squeak, but I grabbed his ankle and tripped him up. When he was down, I quickly stood. I went to run to my daughter, wondering where Josh was, but I wasn't fast enough. He grabbed my wrist and brought me close to him. My back hit his chest, his hand wound around my throat.

"Mum," Nary yelled.

At that moment the front door smashed in and five men ran in with guns out, pointed directly at Oscar and myself.

I caught the sob before it escaped.

I knew those men.

I had met them that afternoon.

"Move the fuck away from her and we won't hurt you," Talon, Zara's man, ordered.

"No!" Oscar bellowed. "Stay where you are and I won't take her life right now." He applied pressure, causing me to choke on my breath. My hands went to his wrist and I tried pulling him away, but I was losing.

"Do you know who we are, motherfucker?" Griz growled.

"No, and I don't give a fuck. I came here for one thing and I have to get it."

"Talon?" Stoke asked.

Stoke...Declan Stoke. The one man who I wished hadn't been there. He sent my heart wild and made my body tingle. He was more dangerous than the situation I was in, with his steel-coloured eyes and dark brown hair.

"Not yet," Talon replied.

"You leave here without the thing you want or there will be hell to pay," Killer said.

"She doesn't know what he wants," Nary said.

"Girl, get outta here," Stoke ordered on a glare.

"She doesn't know," Nary pleaded. "He can't have something that Mum can't give him because she doesn't know," she yelled.

"Sounds like the cops are coming," Blue said.

The hand tightened again. He was panicking, in doing so, he put more pressure on my neck. I fought. I wriggled, but he wasn't letting go. Pressure built in my face as I struggled to breathe.

"Stoke," Talon barked.

I watched as Stoke looked back to my daughter and ordered, "Nary, get out of here, now."

"But—"

"Now, Nary!" he yelled and then quieted his tone. "We'll get your mum to you real soon. Go to your brother next door."

I would have thought it sweet he was taking care of my daughter's feelings...if my life wasn't being choked from me.

She took one last look at me, nodded to Stoke and left the room.

When Stoke turned back, his eyes were wild. "Last chance, let her go," he viciously snarled.

"You can't shoot me. You'll get her."

That was when Stoke smirked. "You don't know me." With that, he fired his gun. Oscar's body jerked back. His hand falling from my neck, I stumbled forward into the arms of Killer.

"We got you," he said.

"You shot me," I heard Oscar say with surprise. In the next second, there was glass breaking and Talon was yelling, "After him."

Heavy footsteps sounded around me as Killer helped me to the couch. He sat me down and stood in front of me as I controlled the breath fighting it's was back into my body. The couch depressed as someone sat beside me. I glanced out the corner of my eyes to see Talon there. He took hold of my chin and turned my head gently. With his other hand, he ran it over my cheek where Oscar had hit me.

"Boss." I heard growled.

"Easy, Stoke, I'm just checking."

"The cops are close," Killer announced.

"Malinda," Talon said. When I met his eyes, he added, "Don't talk okay? It will only hurt. We'll do all the talking." He looked over my shoulder and said, "Tell me that's one of Vi's guns?"

"It is," Stoke replied. I knew it was Stoke because, for some reason only my brain would know, his deep voice was lodged into my memory.

Talon let go of me and stood. "Wipe the prints. I'll call Vi and tell her what's going on," he said and walked off into the kitchen.

Someone walked through the front door, but I didn't have the energy to look or care...until I heard that someone being slammed against a wall. My head spun towards the sound, causing me to cringe in pain. Stoke had a big man, just a fraction larger than Stoke's formidable size pinned to my wall just inside the front door, with an arm against the guy's chest.

Near nose-to-nose, Stoke barked, "Where the fuck were you, Pipe?"

"I-I, get the fuck off me," the big guy snapped.

"I said, where the fuck were you?"

"What's going down?" he dumbly asked.

I saw Stoke's body lock before he growled, "You're supposed to watch her. Keep her safe, fucker. Yet we get a call from her frightened daughter saying a man was in the house threatening her mum, and when we get to her, *brother*," he spat, "that man had a hand around Malinda's neck choking the life out of her. So I'll ask you one last time. Where. The. Fuck. Were. You?"

"I had to take a dump."

Stoke visibly pulled back in shock. "You had to take a dump. You—"

"Brother," came a warning from Killer.

"If you need to leave, you know the drill. You call someone in. You stupid fuck." Stoke pushed forward and then moved away, turning his back on Pipe.

"Boss," Pipe said, looking toward the kitchen.

Talon was standing in the doorway with a look of disgust on his face. "Get the fuck outta my sight before the cops get here. We'll deal with you later. Just fuckin' pray it won't be Stoke doin' the dealin'."

"Fuck," Pipe hissed before he walked out the front door.

"Vi's on her way," Talon announced to Killer and Stoke. His eyes moved back to the still open front door and said in an annoyed tone, "Cops are here." He then leaned against the kitchen doorframe, crossing one leg over the other, and his arms over his chest. Killer moved to the door and Stoke moved to sit next to me on the couch.

"Everything will be good. Just go with it, yeah?"

My throat was still tender so I nodded my reply. He sat back and placed his arm along the back of the couch as two police officers stormed into the living room with guns drawn.

"Nobody move," the younger, smaller man yelled. He looked over his shoulder and moved aside. Stepping up behind him was one of the most amazing men I had ever seen.

I say one of the most, because the other one was, right now, sitting tense beside me.

"Riggs, put your gun away, you too, Stanley," the mountain of a man ordered in a rough bedroom voice. He stood just inside the door taking in the room as I took him in. Dressed in jeans and a dark blue shirt, his gun holstered to his side and a black belt that held up his tight jeans had a large cowboy buckle at the front.

I turned my head enough to look out the corner of my eyes to Stoke. He jaw was clenched, his eyes narrowed.

Why, oh, why did I feel as though I was cheating on a man I didn't know, by looking at a fine specimen of man?

What I'd also like to know, was why in the heck I was so calm after the situation I was in?

I could have died.

Oscar was ready to take my life.

If he did, he could have harmed my children.

All over something, I knew nothing about.

Tears filled my eyes as it all hit me.

Great, it was finally hitting me while I was in front of not one, but two men who I didn't want witness to my break down.

A sob tore through my throat. I winced. What I felt first was Stoke's hand grip the back of my neck in a gentle gesture. What I felt next and saw was hot cop-man crouch in front of me, with his hands on his knees. He gave me a tight-mouthed smile. My heart skipped a beat.

"Hey," he said warmly, "I'm detective Lan Davis, before I ask questions, I need to know you're okay?"

That was sweet.

Through watery eyes, I saw his dark blue eyes soften. Mutely, I nodded.

"Good." He nodded and I missed it when he smiled. I missed his perfect, sweet smile because I was too busy looking at his perfect, dark blond, stylish hair.

Cops weren't supposed to be so good-looking.

Which was maybe why he was a detective.

"You can back the fuck off now," Stoke hissed.

Turning my head to Stoke was out of the option since he held the back of my neck in a steady grip. It didn't hurt at all, with the way was he running his thumb up and down the side of my neck gave me comfort. However, I also didn't turn to Stoke because I got the vibe that he was pissed about something and Stoke being pissed was…scary.

Instead, I kept my eyes on Lan and saw the detective turn his head to Stoke and grin, "Declan, good to see you, cousin."

Stoke snorted. "Yeah, fuckin' peachy."

Lan stood from his crouch and turned to Talon. "You want to explain what went down? Why the police get a phone call from Mrs May's daughter telling us her uncle was here and hurting her mother?"

"It's exactly as you said it," Talon answered.

Someone behind me, an officer no doubt, scoffed.

"Okay then, you want to tell me what you three are doing here? And where the perp got to?" He walked further into the living room.

"I can explain that." Looking to the door, I saw a short, slim woman wearing black slacks and a white silk shirt. Behind her was Blue and Griz. I wasn't sure if the detective noticed, but I did as Griz sent a head shake to Talon.

My stomach dropped.

He'd got away.

Oscar was still out there somewhere.

Fuck!

My gaze went to Lan as he snorted and then swore under his breath. "Violet, fancy seeing you here. I'd heard you'd taken your brother back in with open arms. Then again, I also heard you're getting hitched to Travis, the biggest kingpin in Melbourne's prostitute game."

Oh. My. God.

I shifted on the couch to watch Violet's response and I was glad I did when I saw her eye roll. "Get fucked, Lan. My personal life isn't any of your business." She entered the room. Blue and Griz walked off towards the kitchen way to have a quiet word with Talon as Violet came to stand next to Lan. "To answer your first question. Mrs May's daughter, Nary, called Mrs May's—"

"Malinda," I uttered and both turned to me.

"Sorry?" Violet asked.

"Y-you can call me Malinda."

She gave me a small smile. "As I was saying, she called Malinda's friend Matthew, who is Zara's brother, and you know Zara is married to my brother. It just so happens that when she called, we were all at a barbeque, which Malinda had been to earlier that day. So when Nary called Matthew, I came over, you know, just in case the police didn't arrive in time." She smirked. "I came with these men here. When we entered, Oscar May, Malinda's brother-in-law had her over there," she pointed to the spot near the television, "with his hand around her throat. We could tell she was losing consciousness so I took matters into my own hands. To save the life of Malinda, I shot him once in the arm. He jumped out of the window and that was when I, with Blue and Grady, pursued him. Unfortunately, he got away."

The lies fell easily from Vi's mouth as I sat there and watched on. Worry marred my thoughts for the fact she was lying to a detective. However, I wasn't fazed by it, if it hadn't been for those bikers, I wouldn't be alive and Nary's life would have been in the balance as well.

CHAPTER FIVE

STOKE

I watched as Malinda closed her eyes. I knew she'd seen the look shared between Griz and Talon, so she knew he'd escaped. But hearing it made it real. My thumb continued to stroke her neck. She opened her eyes and looked up at me. I sent her a reassuring smile, but she quickly looked away. I wasn't sure what that was about, but she didn't move away from my hold, so I stayed close to make sure she knew she wasn't alone.

She wouldn't be, not until we got that fucker.

Pipe was a motherfucking moron. There was no doubt about it, he was going to fucking pay for not doing his job right.

"Malinda," my arsehole of a cousin said.

She opened her eyes and looked up.

"How's your throat, honey?"

She took a breath and opened her mouth. "S-sore," she whispered.

"Don't fuckin' make her talk, you dick. Just ask her yes and no questions, then get the fuck outta here," I growled.

Lan glared down at me. I wanted him to bite back. I wanted him to make an idiot out of himself. But he didn't, the arse.

Instead, he crouched down in front of Malinda and laid a hand on her knee. I wanted to fuckin' rip his arm from his body and beat him over the head with it. Then maybe shove it up in arse for good measure. However, because it was Goddamn illegal, I didn't. Instead, I stared daggers down at it instead.

"Malinda," he started, I was sure that was out of protocol. *Shouldn't he be calling her by her surname?* "Do you know why Oscar May was here?"

I snorted. Of course she fucking didn't. Lan glared at me, but quickly turned soft eyes back to my woman as she shook her head. I gave her neck a squeeze.

Christ. My woman. Seriously?

Hell, I'd think about that bold, motherfucking statement later, when my Goddamn cousin wasn't poaching on my territory.

And there I go again. Jesus.

"Does Oscar come here often?" Lan asked.

She shook her head.

"Were Oscar and your husband close?"

She held out her hand and shifted it from side to side, meaning sort of.

"I need to explain something to you, Malinda, and I don't think you will like it." He waited for her nod. "I have been watching Oscar May for some time now. We believe he has been in some trouble with Anthony Graham. Do you know who that is?"

She didn't. I could see in on her face. But as soon as that name left my cousin's mouth, I stiffened, causing Malinda's eyes came to me. She'd felt it. We stared at each other for a moment. She was studying my face, then she turned back to Lan and shook her head.

Lan nodded. "I believe Oscar has been working for Anthony, however, recently some… things Anthony was supposed to get didn't show. Malinda, Anthony Graham is one of the lead mobster bosses in Melbourne. He runs many underground things. He's mean, ruthless and nasty. You would never want to be on his bad side, however recently, Oscar slid right onto his bad side in a big way. Whatever Oscar wants from you, I have reason to believe it's what Anthony is after from him. I also believe… and I'm sorry to say, that your husband was also involved. Which is why we believe the item Oscar is looking for, that will save his life, is here, in your house."

I wanted to punch Lan in the fucking face for causing Malinda to reel in heavy and hard thoughts. I didn't like it her stressed.

Strong goddamn feelings were overriding me. Why was there a need to protect a woman I hardly knew? She was a brother's wife for fuck's sake.

The feelings sucked arse.

I needed to step back.

"Do you mind if we searched your home, Malinda?" Lan asked.

Fuck.

My gut clenched.

She looked devastated as she stared blankly at my cousin.

"Tomorrow," I barked. "Enough for tonight, cousin. She needs rest. She needs to think and take all the shit you just spewed in. So tomorrow, I'm sure Malinda will let you lot through." I sat forward and released her neck to catch her eyes. Once she turned to me, I said, "You'll allow that, yeah, love?"

She nodded and again I saw there was no thought in it. I honestly didn't even think she knew what she was agreeing to.

"Okay, let's get you to your kids." At my words, she blinked life back into her eyes. Widening, she nodded twice. Lan moved out of the way as she stood. I quickly stood next to her.

With my hand on her elbow, I started to walk her to the kitchen. There was no way I wanted her walking out the front for the neighbours to see her in that state.

"Declan," Lan called. I stopped us both and looked over my shoulder. "I need a word. Is there someone else to take her?"

"Killer, Blue?"

Killer was the first to answer. "Sure, brother." He strode toward us and soon had Malinda swept out the back door off the kitchen, with Blue for backup. Fuck... I wanted to be the one to go with her; to see her to her kids safely.

Lan ordered the officers out to their car while he stayed, and I moved back to Lan and Vi. Talon and Griz walked with me to join the huddle.

"The only reason I told that information to Malinda in front of you, is because I think she will need all the help she can get. She'll need to be watched twenty-four seven. Not only her, her kids as well. I could take her into protective custody, but even that won't be safe enough. Not only do we have this shit to deal with, but there's a leak in the department. Anthony had a hard-on for Oscar. He wants him and wants him bad. I don't know how Oscar keeps escaping Anthony's thugs, but he has. Which un-fucking-fortunately means it's no doubt brought attention to Malinda's doorstep."

Talon nodded. "We'll do whatever's needed. She's one of ours. She'd been married to a member, you know that."

"Yeah, I also know that fourteen years ago Malinda went to the hospital with two broken ribs, a fractured cheekbone, bruises and cuts."

"Was she in an accident? Why are you telling us this?" Violet asked a question we all wanted to.

"She said she fell down the stairs at home." He waited and looked around to all of us. With an eye roll, he added, "Do you see any stairs here?"

"Fuck," I uttered. Rage filled me.

Griz and Talon's jaws clenched.

"How do we not know this?" I growled. "How the fuck do we not know a brother was married and dealing in shit."

"It's not like we live in each other's pockets, brother," Griz said.

"Tank was always at the compound. Always the one to party hard with the clubs whores. Fuckin' hell!" Talon cursed. He was taking it badly. Christ, it wasn't only him. Tank had been a brother and none of us knew shit about him. None of us knew what the fucker had done, to not only his life, but his family.

If we had known any of it, we would've stopped it. We would've stopped him.

How the fuck could he lay down with a whore when he had Malinda at home?

"I'd heard their marriage hadn't been the same since," Lan said

Talon snorted. "You can say that again. I doubt he was even around."

"She'll be reserved against all bikers."

Nodding, I said, "We've already seen it."

"Goddamn lucky we have Julian. Malinda was even standoffish with the women."

"Julian could get a wild animal to like him." Violet smiled.

"So you're agreeing to watch out for Malinda?" Lan asked.

"It was going to happen whether you liked it… or not," I said.

Lan sighed. "Okay, cousin." He turned his attention to Violet. "I'm going to need to check the gun you used to shoot Oscar, just to make sure, of course, that it was your weapon and no one else's. Seems you are the only one who has a bloody permit to carry a gun."

"Of course, you'll find it on the coffee table."

He looked from Violet to the table. He studied the gun there for a moment. He knew it wasn't Violet who shot it. We could see it from the amused expression he held. Still, he wiped that clean and turned back to us. "Glad you arrived in time, Violet."

"So am I," she said.

"Right," Talon started, "we need to move to make things safe for Malinda. Keep us in the loop, detective, and we'll do the same."

Lan sent him a chin lift, bagged the gun and walked from the house. Turning to Talon, I asked, "What's the plan?"

"We need a safe place for Malinda and her kids. We need to find fuckin' Oscar before the cops get him, and we'll need to have a meet with Anthony."

"She'll want to stay here with the kids," Violet said, I had that same feeling.

"Fuck, it'd probably be the best bet. We can get Warden in to rig up a security system. We can have men here around the clock. We need to keep things relative normal for her kids as well. They've been through enough shit as is." Griz said.

"I think that's a good idea." I nodded. "We'll need at least four brothers on roster, they'll change every eight hours and then two more at the kids' school."

"Let's get this shit done then. Stoke, go get Malinda and her kids. I'll make some calls while Griz and Vi clean this shit up. We'll get a window guy here tomorrow. I'll get Pick, Dodge, Bull and Limp here for the first shift."

"I'm crashing on the couch until the window's fixed," I

announced. Talon shared a look with Griz; their damn lips twitched. "Don't even fuckin' start," I growled.

I WALKED to Malinda's next-door neighbour's two-story house. Killer was waiting out the front. I told him what the plan was and then he fucking smirked. "Blue's out back. I'll go let him know. We'll wait out here until our brother's show. You get them home. They're all tired on their feet."

Sending him a chin lift, I opened the front door as Killer called and added, "Good luck in there. If you think Nancy's bad, she's nothing compared to Mrs Cliff." He chuckled as I stumbled over the threshold.

Fuck.

"Holy shit, you're bigger than the other two. Are you on steroids?" a scratchy voice barked.

Motherfucker! The word ran through my head as I closed the door behind me and turned back around.

"What's your name? The other two had funny names. Who in their right mind would call their child Blue or Killer? What in the hell's that? So, what's yours and what're you gonna do for my sweet Malinda?" She stood in the doorway of her living room, which would lead to other parts of her house, her hands on her round hips and a robe covering them. To complete the picture of the woman before me, her green hair was in rollers and a smoke was hanging out of her mouth. She looked every bit the no-bull-shit old woman.

"I'm Stoke and we have everything under control. I've come to take Malinda and her kids home."

"Jesus, Stoke, really?" She rolled her eyes. "Okay, I guess I have to believe you. But if you and the other guys don't do a good job, I'm gonna have to bring my boys in."

I seriously had to wonder who her boys were.

"Glad to see Malinda has a good neighbour," I offered.

"Don't you try and sweet talk me. You're damn fine, but I won't have you wooing me with your charm."

A smirk filled my lips. Yes, she was worse than Nancy, Wildcat's mum.

"Can I grab Malinda and the kids, or are you gonna stand there and question me more?"

"I think I like you. You've got spunk. The other two soon cleared out of the house. I reckon they're scared of me, but you're willing to stand there in your sex-god form and have a chat." She studied me. "You want a coffee?"

Christ. "I'll have to take a rain check. I'm sure Malinda and her kids are dog tired and need some rest."

"Yep, you'll do." She grinned, her smoke nearly falling from her mouth.

"I'll do for what?" I questioned, not sure I should have.

"My sweet Malinda." She took a couple of steps forward and uttered, "You need to give her a bit of hanky-panky." She winked. "You know what I mean. She could go a few rounds in the sheets with you."

"Mrs Cliff," Nary called. She came around the corner and saw I was standing there. She blushed and looked to the ground. "Um, my mum has had all of her drink. Does she need more?"

55

"No, sweet child," Mrs Cliff answered. Turning back to me, she continued, "I gave her my special concoction. Should fix her throat up real good, it'll be fine by morning." She looked to Nary and added, "Go get your momma, child. Tell her that her man's here to take you all home."

"I'm not—"

"I'll go get her," Nary said with a smile before she left.

Mrs Cliff rolled her eyes and scoffed. "I'm sure you wish."

CHAPTER SIX

MALINDA

I woke in the middle of the night gasping for breath. Fright bombarded my mind, until I reassured myself I was safe. However, I was left feeling frustrated. Flinging the sheets off, I moved to sit on the edge of the mattress and held my neck. Stupid bloody Oscar. How dare he invade my precious sleep. Great, I was going to be cranky for the rest of the day. I always was if I didn't get my usual eight hours of sleep.

My mind drifted over the horror.

I had never been scared like that before in my life, not even when Tank took his hand to me. However, it was more of the fact I wasn't scared for myself; I was petrified for my children. Thankfully, Nary had been smart enough to stay quiet when she heard the commotion. She quickly and quietly shuffled Josh out the back door and told him to get to Mrs Cliff's. Nary told me everything as soon as I showed up next door. Josh hadn't wanted to leave at first, until Nary threatened him that she'd show her video of him dancing around our house in his boxers to his friends at school. Nary reassured him she would call the police. She had of course, but first she called Mattie. Thank goodness she did, the police would have been too late and I could have lost my daughter, as well as my life.

That thought alone churned my stomach and brought tears to my eyes.

Once I showed up to Mrs Cliff's and she opened the door to not only me but also Killer and Blue. She took them in, smiled, introduced herself and threatened them to keep me and my children safe. This was while she took me into her arms for a hug. After that, she made fun of their names and told them they were too pretty for names that foolish. It was lucky Nary and Josh came running from the back of the house to defuse the situation. When Killer and Blue quickly fled the house to guard the front and back outside, she took me and my children, who were attached to me as tightly as I was to them, into the kitchen.

In there, as Nary told me her side, Mrs Cliff made me drink. It was something that tasted like old unwashed socks. Josh had moved his chair close to my side and took my hand in his, and as Nary spoke, she had her hand on my knee. They were both worried about me, not only because I could hardly speak, but because of the whole fucked-up situation.

Damn Oscar to hell.

When Stoke had turned up, I was grateful. Not only was I physically tired, but emotionally as well.

Without words spoken, I followed him back to my house to see Talon, Griz and Vi still there. They had cleaned the house and fixed the window for the night, informing me a glazer was coming the next day to repair it properly. They also told me, after I saw the children to bed, that they organised someone to come by to install a security system in the house.

My shoulders slumped in relief when I realised we were able to stay in our house. I didn't want to have to move the children. I didn't want to worry them more than they already were.

Before Talon and his men left, after they mentioned Stoke was sleeping on the couch and I had a quiet panic attack, I tried to thank them. Until Talon came forward and laid one finger on my lips. What he said brought tears to my eyes. "Even if you weren't Tank's, we'd do this. My woman has taken a liking to you, if I didn't do this, she'd kick my arse. You're Hawks, Malinda. You just need to get used to it."

When they left, I turned to Stoke as he ordered, "Try to get some sleep." I gestured to the couch and he clipped, "I'll find the shit for it. Just get to bed, woman."

I had studied him, mainly because my eyes really didn't want to look away. Only I had to. I nodded and retreated to my room where I had a shower so I could cry in peace. After the water turned cold, I dressed into panties and a nightie, crawled into bed and fell asleep right away.

I looked to the clock on my bedside table. It read one am. I'd been asleep for only two hours.

My mind was playing funny buggers. It wanted to relive the event over and over.

Relive the hand around my throat.

Relive the fright in my daughter's eyes.

Oh, God, she'd been so brave.

Wiping my eyes, I stood and made my way down the hall, through the living room, and into the kitchen to pour myself a glass of water to cool my throat. After drinking it, I walked back into the living room and stopped.

For a moment, just a moment, I had forgotten Stoke was there.

However, the sight before me was now burned into my mind. There was a dim light from the street lamppost shining in through the large bay window. I could easily make out a shirtless Stoke laying on the couch with a blanket around his waist, his arms were up over his head. His muscled body was bulging. Unfortunately, his face was turned toward the couch and in shadow; I couldn't see it.

So I jumped when his voice rumbled, "Can't sleep?"

"B-bad dream," I uttered. Relief washed through me as my throat didn't hurt when I talked.

He turned his head; his steel-coloured eyes pinned me to my spot. "Come here, Malinda."

My eyes widened. My pulse picked up and I shook my head.

"Malinda," he growled low. "Come here."

Maybe he wanted to talk without waking the children, so I took the couple of steps forward and stopped just beside the couch.

"Yes?" I asked.

He didn't answer. He just looked up at me, and then in the next second, he reached out a hand, wrapped one around my wrist and I was pulled forward. He quickly shifted and I landed with my bottom in the crook of his hip. I scrabbled up, well, tried to, but his vice-grip on my wrist tightened. He moved again and tugged me down so I was laying in front of him on the couch. My heart was going crazy behind my ribs, wondering what Stoke wanted.

I attempted to sit up, since he no longer held my wrist, but his arm quickly surrounded my waist and he snapped, "Rest."

"But—"

"Malinda, just go to sleep."

"B-but—"

"I'm tired. You're tired. All we're gonna to do is sleep."

"The children, if they see me here in the morning...."
They'd get ideas.

"I'll wake before they do and get you to your room."

"But—"

"Just sleep, woman."

Sighing, I slumped back into his heat. "Okay," I whispered to the room. His arm around my waist gave me a squeeze. I didn't think I would be able to sleep, but I did. I think what helped was the warmth from Stoke's amazing body and the fact I felt safe in his arms.

I woke to find myself in my bed. How I got back there I didn't know. All I remembered was falling to a dreamless sleep against Stoke. A smile tugged at my lips, but I fought it back. Even if one of the most handsome men I had ever seen held me while I slept, to comfort me from my bad dream...there was nothing to smile about. I had lost a husband. A husband whose bullshit and deception was leaking into my house, seeping into my life and my children's. Touching my throat with my fingers, I gently cleared it with a small cough. It felt ninety percent better. Mrs Cliff's disgusting concoction worked a miracle. She should go into business.

Once out of bed, I washed up before donning my bathrobe and went to look for my children.

Finding them in the kitchen was normal on a school morning. However, I decided last night they weren't going, so when I spotted them dressed and ready for school, I was surprised.

What I was also surprised about was that Stoke was standing shirtless leaning against the wooden kitchen bench, sipping coffee while Josh told him all about last night as if he hadn't been there.

"Morning, Mum," Nary said from the kitchen table as she scoffed down cereal.

"Morning, honey." I smiled.

"Hey, Mum. Did you know Stoke stayed here last night to protect us and that we'll have other biker guy's keeping an eye out for us in case our dick uncle comes back?" Josh beamed.

From a wide-eyed stare at my son, I turned them to Stoke and narrowed them. "Josh, language," I snapped, and then said to Stoke, "A word, please." With that, I spun on my heels and started for the living room, only to turn back around and tell the children, "Guys, go get changed. You won't be going to school today."

"Awesome," Josh yelled. Nary leaned back in her chair and turned her gaze from me to Stoke, so I looked to Stoke.

"They should go," he stated.

"No, they shouldn't," I snapped. "Were you the one to tell them to dress in their school clothes?"

"Yes." He smiled. "I was also the one who woke them up and got them ready for school because they should go."

"They had a traumatic weekend, Declan Stoke. I think they need to stay home." Why did his eyes suddenly flare my way?

"They need to get back into the swing of things, Malinda. They need to learn that life goes on, even if trouble is brewing. They know you'll have Hawks at your backs. Nothing will happen to 'em."

I had an urge to stamp my foot and yell at him. Instead, my body tensed, my hands clenched at my sides and I scowled.

"It's okay, Mum," Josh said. "Stoke's right. School will be good for us."

Shaking my head to clear it, I turned my shocked eyes to my son. A son who would pretend to be sick to get a day off school. I looked to Nary, who apparently found this whole scene amusing.

What was wrong with my children?

"Still, honey," I started quietly. "Something at school could upset you or you could relive last night at any moment. I want you home for that."

"Mum." Josh snorted and rolled his eyes. "We'll be fine. Stoke's gonna have men at school and all. Isn't that freakin' awesome?"

Jesus Christ on crackers. He'd brainwashed my children.

Through clenched teeth, I hissed, "Yeah, baby. Awesome."

"Kids, go brush your teeth and pack your bags. A brother will be here soon to take you both to school," he ordered with a smug smile upon his sinful, sexy face. A face I had a sudden impulse to smack.

"Unreal," Josh breathed and ran from the room.

Nary stood from the table, walked to the sink, where Stoke was standing, and placed her bowl in. Stoke turned to her and asked, "You cool with school, girl?"

A grin filled her lips. "Yeah, Stoke," she said and walked my way. "It'll be fine, Mum," she added, then gave me a kiss on the cheek before she walked out.

A minute ticked by as I stood there in my robe, with my arms crossed over my chest. Glaring up at Stoke, who remained leaning his cute arse against the bench, as he sipped his fucking coffee while his lips twitched.

"Coffee?" he asked.

I growled low and he laughed. "Sure, Stoke, I'll have a coffee in my house, from my kettle, in a mug that's in my cupboard, while I guess you can go and organise *my* children."

I wanted to squeak out a scared sound and flee the room as all amusement left his face. He put his coffee cup down and stalked toward me. When he was close, close enough for me to feel his heat, he leaned down, his lips grazed my ear. "I like your attitude, woman, but I fuckin' loved it when you called me Declan more. You call me Stoke again, you'll be over my lap and soon find your arse sore from my hand. Now, love, you need to learn that Hawks will have your back. Even if that means dealin' with your children while you slept, because you needed to rest." He pulled back and looked down at me. "They'll be fine Malinda, if they aren't, then we'll deal." With that, he stalked from the room, only to call over his shoulder, "I'm going for a shower before my brothers get here."

Oh. My.

Fury ran through my veins, what also ran alongside it was gratitude. He wanted to take care of things while I rested. He wanted to help me out.

I hadn't had that for such a long time.

What also flushed through my body was heat from his words. His body was smoking hot, but when his breath brushed across my ear, speaking those words, his hotness level reached supernova. I fanned myself down trying my hardest not to imagine him in my shower…naked.

I failed.

AFTER HAVING a quick coffee to calm my thoughts, I wanted to get dressed. As Stoke walked from my adjoining bathroom—not the children's which was the more commonly used one by guests—looking delectable in jeans, a black fitted tee and bare feet, I knew I was in danger of ogling him and probably humiliating myself by drooling. So I made a quick escape to my room to get dressed.

I didn't want bikers showing up with me still in a robe. It was already enough Stoke had eyed me up when I stood in front of him in the kitchen. When I saw his eyes roaming my body, I'd looked away quickly, wishing I was wearing something sexier. *No, stupid libido. Sexy is bad.* It was safer being almost a mirror image of Mrs Cliff in my frumpy robe. All I needed was to dye my hair green, put it in rollers, then we could be twins.

I made it out to the living room as Stoke opened the front door. "Hey," he greeted. They gave a chin lift to Stoke, but quickly turned their gaze to me. I bit my bottom lip as they studied me from head to toe. Uncomfortable, I shifted on my feet wondering if I'd entered a parallel universe and perhaps had walked out naked. I looked down at myself to double check, making sure I had in fact put on my black leggings and a long floaty top which covered my bottom, but was a little tight across my double Ds.

"Um, hi," I offered with a wave.

The man with the hard gaze and massive body looked from me, to Stoke, back to me, and back to Stoke, then snapped, "You fuckin' lucky bastard."

Huh? Stoke's lucky? About what? That he stayed in the house?

Stoke then smiled an arrogant smile.

The other one who was smiling at me stepped through the door and walked to me with his hand held out. "Hey, I'm Warden. I'm here to do your security. If anything else you need done arises, I'm more than willing to help out—" he said, holding my hand in his much larger one. He was bigger than Stoke or even Griz.

"Warden," Stoke warned.

"I'm also not a Hawks member. I work with Violet. I'm a PI, baby. Just keep that in mind." He grinned, kissing my hand he was still holding. That was until Stoke came up and knocked Warden to the side. If Stoke didn't quickly place his arm around my waist, I would have stumbled along with Warden, who was now laughing.

"So easy to fuck with you guys."

"Yo, kids," Stoke yelled. Warden laughed harder, and Dodge, I think his name was I'd heard it mentioned at the barbeque, chuckled with him. Josh came around the corner first and stopped when he spotted Warden. His eyes widened.

"Wow,"

"Hey, little dude." Warden smiled, holding out his fist for a fist bump. Josh gave him one and asked Stoke, "Is he taking us to school?"

"No, kid." Stoke gestured with his chin over to the door. "That's Dodge. He'll be dropping you and your sister off. Two others are already there checking the place out. They'll bring you home after school."

"Awesome." He beamed and headed for Dodge. "Hey," he said with his own chin lift.

Oh, God.

"What's up, little guy."

"Not much," Josh said.

"Josh," I called.

He turned back to me and whined, "Mum."

"Josh." I glared at my son.

"Mum," Josh snapped and shook his head.

Stoke leaned in to my ear. "Love, you can't expect a boy his age to come and kiss him mum goodbye while other brothers are hanging around and be witness to it."

"See! Stoke totally gets it," Josh yelled.

Crossing my arms over my chest, I glared up at Stoke and snapped, "Fine." Even though I hated it, I understood it.

"Nary, get your arse moving," Josh called.

Before I could even open my mouth, Stoke barked, "Language, kid."

"Whoops, sorry, mum," Josh apologised. My son. My fourteen-year-old son apologised because he swore. Usually, he'd say nothing. Maybe give me an eye roll, but he'd say nothing.

Was Stoke a child tamer?

He couldn't be. He freaked the hell out when he was handed a baby.

That was it. He was good with older children, but when it came to a baby, he'd break out in a sweat.

Nary coming into the living room broke through my thoughts. She came up to me and kissed me on the cheek. "See you later, Mum."

I smirked up at Stoke. He laughed and said, "It's different for girls."

"See ya, Stoke."

"Later, girl."

"Bye, babies. Have a good day," I called. "If you need me, just call, okay."

"Sure, Mum," Nary said with a grin and closed the front

door behind her. Josh had already bounded down the steps with Dodge.

Stoke gave my waist a squeeze.

It was then I realised that the whole time I was saying goodbye and talking, I was standing with Stoke at my side with his arm around me, and my children didn't seem fazed by it at all.

Oh. My.

That was not good.

CHAPTER SEVEN

TWO WEEKS LATER

MALINDA

*T*ime seemed to be speeding up for me. Fourteen days had passed. Thankfully, it had been uneventful. Well, uneventful in a way that no one tried to harm my family. However, it had been eventful in other ways, and one way had just walked into the kitchen.

"Stoke," Josh yelled as he stood. "You made it." He proceeded to do some sort of manly handshake.

"Hey, girl," Stoke said as he passed Nary sitting at the table. I watched as he gave her shoulder a squeeze and moved on.

"Hi, Stoke. You on duty tonight?" Nary asked.

"Sure am." He grinned as he continued to walk around the bench. He walked up to my side and kissed my cheek, "Hey, love, what's for dinner."

Every time over the fourteen days, he'd walked into my house as if he owned it, like he lived here, and asked me the same question. And each time, I had to still my rapid heart.

"Homemade pizza tonight," I informed him while watching him head to the fridge and grab himself a can of coke.

He spun around, popped the top, but before he chugged it down, like he always did, he grinned over at me and said, "Sounds awesome."

Oh. My.

I loved his smiled. A smile I was becoming increasingly familiar with, even though every time he shared it with me, it made me want to melt into a puddle of goo. Instead, I sent him a small grin and turned back to the chopping board to pick up where I'd left off before he entered.

The day after Stoke stayed the night, the day after the event and my children left for school, I avoided Stoke like the plague. My emotions and thoughts were driving me insane. I couldn't believe I had felt that relaxed in Declan's arms as I said goodbye to my children. I couldn't believe I hadn't even taken it in and protected my own children's thoughts of what they may have been thinking... God, I wasn't even sure if *that* made sense.

He'd given me that day. He stayed clear as Warden installed the security system. Okay, so I had mostly stayed in my room until lunchtime and my stomach howled in anger. I also felt bad that I was acting foolish. I went out and fed Warden, since Declan wasn't in sight. I talked and laughed with Warden. He was a nice man to get to know, in the end, while he finished what he had to do, I stuck by him and kept him entertained with stories of the children and just plain old chatter.

But then Warden climbed down off his ladder and stood on the porch looking down at me, where I sat on the old rickety swing chair. He suddenly announced, "He's a good dude."

I was surprised by his outburst, we had just been talking about football teams, so I asked, "Who?"

He smirked. "Stoke."

"Um… that's nice."

Warden rolled his eyes and sat next to me. "He's loyal as well. I've never known a brother to be that devoted. So loyal he took a bullet to the gut helping a brother. So bloody loyal he took a beating while trying to protect another brother's woman."

Oh, God. My body shivered from the thought of Declan hurt. He was all-male and so truehearted.

I hadn't taken noticed of any scarring the night before.

"He's a good guy, Mally," Warden said, using the nickname he gave me. "The ones I know in the Hawks club are. I don't know all of them, most, but not all. So I didn't know your ex—"

"He wasn't my ex, Warden."

Warden sighed. "I'm sorry, Mally, but I think if you're totally honest with yourself, he kinda was. Vi knows shit. She can find a lot out and I'm sorry, but I'm one of her men, so she tells me shit. You and your husband hadn't really been a couple for some time. All I want you to know is that…what you're feeling when you look at Stoke, it's okay to feel that. It's okay to be attracted to him."

"Warden," I warned. I couldn't… I wouldn't… I wasn't ready for that.

"That's all I'll say, Mally. Now, get me a drink, woman. I'm dying of thirst."

I smiled up at him. I took his hand as tears filled my eyes and said, "Thank you, honey."

"Damn, don't let Stoke hear you call me that. I'll get my arse kicked."

I laughed because I highly doubted it.

But I had been wrong, and that didn't come about until three nights later. I hadn't seen Stoke in those two nights. He'd kept his distance. Once he had a shift at the children's school and dropped them home, he didn't come in, not until the next night.

The police had been there that day to go through my house, searching for whatever Oscar thought was there. Only they came up with nothing. The day before I had been to the police station to give my statement, as well as put a restraining order out against Oscar.

Oscar had disappeared into thin air. However, the Hawks members and the police were sure he'd still try something. Which was why we were still under surveillance. There was also the tension surrounding Anthony Graham, who was refusing to take a meet with Talon to sort out the issue regarding me.

So I was surprised that when I was on the phone to Warden, who was becoming a fast friend, that Stoke walked through the back door off the kitchen. My eyes widened when he stalked in and headed straight up to me. He boxed me in, an arm on each side of me, on the bench I was leaning against.

"I, um… I have to go, honey," I said into the phone and Stoke's whole body tensed.

I heard Warden's rumble of laughter on the other end, and then he said, "My guess is that Stoke's there. I heard he was coming tonight. Have fun, Mally."

"Uh-huh," was all I said before Stoke took the phone out of my hand, hung up and placed it on the bench. He leaned in, his arms surround me again and hissed, "Who are you callin' honey?"

"Um… Warden," I whispered as I looked into his hard steel eyes.

"I don't like it, Malinda."

"W-what?"

"You callin' a man honey. I suggest you stop."

"Um… okay?"

"Jesus," he cursed, and then grasped the back of my hair and brought my lips to his, where he continued to surprise me by kissing me with so much passion. Passion I had never felt before, even from Tank when we'd first met. He pulled away and I was sure my head tried to follow him because my lips hadn't had enough.

Then I opened my eyes and uttered, "W-what was that?"

He grinned down at me. "That was me showing you I'm interested, it was also me telling you I don't like you callin' other men honey."

"Oh," I uttered because my brain wasn't functioning.

He chuckled. "Yeah, oh, now I'm stayin' for dinner and sleepin' on the couch again."

"Um… all right?"

He laughed. "I see I'm gonna need to give you some space to think. I'm gonna go see what your kids are doin'." With that, he gave me a quick peck and left the room.

I blinked.

And blinked again.

He was going to see what the children were doing.

He was interested.

Showing me he was interested… in me? That was what he meant… yes?

He didn't want me to call any other man honey.

Stoke was interested in *me*.

Declan Stoke was interested and he showed me in the best way possible.

Only, it all freaked me out.

I'd only buried my husband three days earlier. Even though Warden was right, Tank and I hadn't been in a relationship in a long time, it was still hard to comprehend at the time.

Laughter rang out from the hallway where the children were with Stoke.

Because he was seeing what they were doing.

He was interested.

Yes, all of that, everything about it was going to take a large amount of time to get used to.

Since then, that first kiss, he had been to dinner at my house every second day. He'd slept on the couch every second night and kissed my cheek, just my cheek, every time he walked in.

That was all.

He never made any other move.

Inevitably, I was confused.

He made my kids, and I have to admit myself, laugh a lot. He made us all feel at ease and smile. Declan Stoke wormed his way into our home and our hearts. It was already obvious the children adored him.

I was still out on the matter.

He was amazing with the children, even helped with their homework if he arrived in time for it.

I liked him.

Really, I did, and my heart had warmed. But it also warmed for Warden, Mattie and Julian. So was the warmth for Declan different for the others?

I was unsure.

Regardless, I wished he'd kiss me again. Maybe then, my mind would be made up. Then again, as soon as that thought ran through my mind, guilt hit me.

I was still fighting with myself on so many levels.

Nary and Josh loved having Stoke visit. They loved that he took time out for them, so I was worried that when it ended, how they would react. I was also concerned that as soon as all the crap was over, he would be over with us as well.

Actually, I was terrified about it.

Because of the kids, of course… and nothing else.

No other reason at all.

That was right. I didn't mind if he was done with us at

the end. I didn't mind I would lose his smile, his humour, his kindness, his smokin' hot body to ogle at. Or when he called me love, when he said my name if he was angry, annoyed or in a sweet mood.

I didn't mind at all.

My body jolted back into the present when his hand threaded around my side to stop on my stomach. "You're mind seems to be tickin' over a lot tonight," he whispered into my ear.

Barely containing my gasp, I couldn't still the shudder. He hadn't done that in the last two weeks.

He hadn't shown this closeness in front of the children since that first day.

"Um... yes," I answered.

"Hope its good thoughts, love. If not, I can provide some good ones."

"Uh... okay?"

He chuckled and nuzzled his nose against my neck. "Maybe later, yeah?"

"Ah... maybe?"

His snort touched my skin and then he left his lips there. I closed my eyes, only to open them seconds later when he moved. He went to sit at the dining room table with my children. "Okay, what're we learning tonight?" he asked.

Josh went straight into talking about some math problem, but I noticed Nary wasn't even looking at Stoke. No, she was looking at me, studying me.

I wasn't sure what was going through her head, but she gave me a sweet, small smile and—heck—a thumbs up.

Before I could respond to her thumbs up, there was a

commotion at the front door, followed by a yelled, "You let me in there. No one stops me from doing shit. You best tell your boss that."

"Fuck," Stoke hissed.

"Declan," I snapped as Josh laughed and Nary grinned big.

He turned to face me. "Love, Mrs Cliff is a nut."

A giggle fell from my lips. "I know that, but she's harmless."

"Yeah, unless you have a dick."

"Declan," I snapped again.

"Babe, she thinks all of us want a piece of her arse. She flirts and then yells at us. She's up in our grill all the time, threatening she'll bring her boys in if we don't sort your shit soon. Whoever her fuckin' boys are."

"Declan Stoke, watch your language around my children," I yelled.

He gave me an eye roll, stood and came at me. I was in his arms next and he was looking down at me. "Love, I'm a biker. I curse because it's in my blood to do it. Your kids are old enough to know this and they're also old enough to know that if I hear a swear word outta their mouths, then they have to deal with me. Right, kids?"

"Sure do, Stoke," Josh said.

"Yeah, Stoke," Nary replied.

When and how did that happen?

Okay, so I had noticed over the two weeks the children were bonding with Stoke, but it was because he was making time for them to do that. I also noticed Stoke correcting Josh if he did swear. Also if Nary would start on one of her rants, all Stoke had to do was say her name and she'd stop. Why didn't they do that for me?

Though, I think I knew the answer. Because I also felt the same way.

Declan Stoke was amazing when he was in the mood. But if you pissed him off, he became a scary man and they sensed this. However, we knew he wouldn't lay a finger on us because after we witnessed a time he did lose it, he sat us down and explained it.

He took time out to clarify how he was.

The night we witnessed it was four nights ago when a biker brother of his turned up. I think his name was Hose. He showed up with no notice and came to the front door where Nary answered it. I was sitting on the couch next to Stoke because he planted my bottom there and Josh was sitting next to me. As soon as Nary opened the door, Hose yelled, "Where the fuck is Stoke?"

Stoke was off the couch in seconds and at the front door pushing Nary aside. "Motherfucker, what the fuck you doin'?"

"I'm sick of this shit. You're never at work now and the rest of us have to pick up your slack all because of some stupid pussy and her crap. I've—"

He got no more words out because Stoke punched him in the face. As Hose was leaning over, Stoke growled low and menacing, "You ever fuckin' come here again spouting shit you know nothing about, we're gonna have more trouble than just a broken nose. You ever speak about Malinda like that again, you'll be breathing through a tube. And you ever yell at her daughter again, you'll need help pissing. I'll talk to Killer who's in fuckin' charge. Not that you need to know that now. Seems your fuckin' fired, arsehole. Now leave." With that, he shut the door and turned to us. Both Nary and I were shocked to say the least. Josh was smiling, wide and proud. What we all weren't, was scared.

Mrs Cliff's yelling continued. "Move out of the way or I'll have your balls in my fist real quick."

"One day my brothers are gonna be too scared to come here because of that woman." Stoke grinned. While I giggled, he went to calm the situation down.

CHAPTER EIGHT

STOKE

*O*pening the front door, I came to a halt when Mrs Cliff fell into my arms. Pick, who was standing opposite her, burst out laughing.

"You need to talk to these bikers. Do I look like a fucking bad person to you? He wasn't going to let me in," she hissed to me and then turned to Pick. "I ain't hiding a gun up my robe and between my legs. I ain't wielding knives in my bloody bra either. Next time, mister," she yelled and pointed to Pick, "next time you let me in or else I'll just make you strip me naked to check me over."

"Mrs Cliff, I asked my brothers to let no one in," I said.

She spun back to me and asked, "Why? You getting it on with my Malinda? If that's the case I'll be sure to go right now. I told you two weeks ago to get in her panties and from the looks of her, you haven't. What's taking you so long? Can you even get it up?"

Pick burst out laughing. He was even bent over holding his stomach.

"I assure you, Mrs Cliff, everything is fuckin' fine in that department. Not that it's any of your business."

"Don't get all snooty," she snapped, shoved past me, and walked into the house.

With a growl, I said, "Do you think Malinda would hate me if I killed her?"

"I heard that, and yes, she would," Mrs Cliff yelled from the kitchen.

"Fuck," I hissed. After Pick wished me well, I closed the front door and started for the kitchen.

It was time to make another move on my woman. I'd kissed Malinda two and a bit weeks ago, then I'd stood back and waited. I waited for her to reach out to me, to show me she wanted me, but she hadn't done either. I knew she was attracted to me, even the brothers had said she watched me when I wasn't looking.

Maybe she was just shy?

Or maybe there was too much shit going on in her head to make a move.

Then again, maybe she just didn't want to.

I'd soon find out. That was if Mrs Fucking Cliff didn't stuff everything up.

We'd got shit all from our informant regarding Anthony and Oscar. As far as we knew, Anthony was after Oscar as well. If only the stupid motherfucking Anthony would take a meet with Talon. He said he'd leave Malinda and her kids alone if she was in the clear and wasn't hiding anything.

We gave him all the information the cops gave us after they searched the place and came up empty. He wasn't satisfied with it. It didn't prove she wasn't in play and had his shit. All we could do was wait; the money and coke had to turn up somewhere.

We just hoped it'd be soon.

If Anthony got cocky and hated waiting and tried something, he knew there'd be war, all charters of Hawks around Australia had been notified if anything went down—we were to go to war with Anthony and his men.

That was something Malinda didn't know. She knew she and her kids had our protection, but she didn't know how far that stretched. Some would say war over a woman was crazy, maybe if Talon didn't have Wildcat he would have said it as well. Not now. Now he was prepared to do what needed to be done, to keep her safe.

Fuck, I was grateful.

I wanted her. Not just to bed either. I wanted to know everything about her. I wanted to reach inside her and take what she could give me. In return, I'd give her my all.

I was fuckin' stupid when I declared to myself I wasn't gonna do another relationship. That thought was fuckin' blown outta the water as soon as I saw Malinda.

It just took me a while to realise it.

Some would say I was pussy whipped like a lot of them.

I just had to hope Malinda might want to try this with

me. I was fucking worried she wasn't over Tank. Even though, many around me said she was.

"Stoke, get your arse in here. Pizza's ready," Mrs Cliff yelled.

I groaned, only to smile when I heard from Malinda, "Mrs Cliff, you shouldn't talk to him like that."

"Pfft, please. See you stick up for him, and you try to tell me you don't want to—"

"Mrs Cliff," Malinda snapped. "The children."

"Yeah, right, forgot about them. Sorry, munchkins."

The kids mumbled a reply. I walked into the kitchen and found a pizza placed on the table. "Smells amazing, love," I commented.

She gave me a small smile as she sat down next to Nary, opposite Josh and myself. Mrs Cliff sat at the end of the six-seater black table.

"Thanks, there's more on the way so eat up," she said.

"Great, I'm starving," Mrs Cliff said.

I looked to Malinda and smirked when she sent me an eye roll.

You could say dinner was amusing as well as delicious. Mrs Cliff kept us all entertained with stories from her days in the army. I wasn't sure if they were real, but fuck, they were funny. After dinner, Mrs Cliff made her escape and the kids went to their rooms to do whatever kids did these days. I was sure Nary would be on the phone and Josh would be playing some type of computer game. I sat on the couch in the corner. Malinda came in and looked at me, the couch and then the TV. I'd flicked it on to some crap movie, not that I was planning to watch anything anyway.

Patience went out the window when Malinda went and sat in the chair to the left of the couch. "Get your cute arse over here, woman."

"Um... I think I forgot to turn off the oven. I'll be back in a second." She stood and went to walk away in a hurry, but I was faster. I got up, took two steps to her, planted my arms around her waist, spun her in my arms, and planted her on the sofa. She gasped when I effortlessly shifted her to lay on her back as I hovered over her.

"W-what are you doing?" She stumbled over her words.

Smiling down at her, I noticed her chest rising and falling in a fast pace. She was nervous. "I wanna make out like a couple of teenagers. You up for that?" There, the ball was in her court now.

"I... um. Maybe we should—"

"Malinda," I growled.

"Yes. I'm okay with that."

"Fuck, love," I uttered before my lips touched hers gently.

I pulled back to take in her reaction when she shocked the shit outta me and said, "Teenagers seem to do it better than that."

Laughter rumbled up and out of me. "Woman let me rock your world. I'll show you that a real man can do it a heap better than some horny teenager."

She smirked. "Well, I'm waiting."

I moaned. I loved that she was in a teasing mood. Touching my tongue to her lips, she jumped and gasped. I ran my tongue along her lower lip and before I went all out, I gently bit down. I was surprised when she sighed in contentment. My mouth moulded to hers and she tilted her head as I deepened the kiss. I slid my hand up and down her side as our lips, mouth and teeth went into an overdrive of frenzy. Her hand moved from my waist down to squeeze my arse, again shocking the shit outta me. I moved my own hand down and brought her leg up and over my hip. With that movement, I was closer to her heated core. I slowly thrust my hips into her. She pulled back and moaned, her neck arching.

"Jesus, love, how long has it been?"

I tumbled backward onto the floor when I heard, "A hell of a long time, obviously." Mrs Cliff stood looking over the couch at us. "You should really lock the front door. Those boys just let anyone in."

"You had better—" I started.

"Mrs Cliff," Malinda yelled as she scrambled off the couch with a bright red face. "Did you forget something?"

"Yeah, I think I left my packet of smokes on the table." She walked to the kitchen and looked in. She turned back and shook her head saying, "Nope, not there. Must be home after all. Well, I'll be off. Let you two get back to what you were doing." She made her way to the front door when Malinda stood in front of me. She must have known I was fucking fuming at the old lady. I was ready to take her out, but knowing my luck, she'd just haunt the shit outta me.

"Night, don't forget to lock the door this time. I'm gonna go talk to the guys."

Christ.

"Goodbye, Mrs Cliff."

"Yep," she answered and then closed the door behind her.

Malinda turned to face me. "Declan—"

"You haven't locked the door yet," was yelled from the other side.

"Fuck me," I growled.

"Well, lock the door and Malinda can help with that." Mrs Cliff cackled.

That was when we both looked at each other and burst out laughing. I went over, locked the door and triple checked it. I didn't want the old woman interfering again. God help my brothers out the front. Malinda was already sitting on the couch, so I sat beside her and brought her close to my side.

"Declan—" she started, but I didn't want her to finish it. I knew what was gonna come outta her mouth and I didn't want to hear it. She was regretting kissing me. But fuck, her body had been screaming for it. I just had to wait for her mind to catch up to her body.

"Have I mentioned I like your house?" I asked.

She relaxed beside me. "No, you haven't."

"It's the bomb, babe. You don't see much wood panelling inside houses these days and your house has it everywhere, walls, and roof. The slate on the floor kick's arse as well."

"Not many like it."

"It's unique, different. Fuckin' awesome."

LILA ROSE

I looked down and caught her smile. "Thanks," she whispered as her mobile on the coffee table in front of us rang. She picked it up looked at it and smiled widely. "Hey, Mattie, how are you?"

Fuck. I groaned silently and laid my head back against the couch. The muffkateers had been hounding me for the last two weeks to let them come over. I'd told then 'hell no' every time. I was surprised with Mattie though, because even though I knew Mattie and Malinda talked nearly every day, he hadn't said a word to her about them. How-fucking-ever, there was only so much a sane man could take from Wildcat and her posse. Especially when Mattie was hooked to the worst of them.

"I'm sorry?" she said. "Um, I don't know. What... hello? Oh, hi, Julian. No, it's not that at all. Yes, of course I like you. It's just... um"

That was when I took the phone from her hand and hissed into it, "What in the fuck do you want, Julian?"

"Oh, hey, Stoke." Goddamn it, I could hear the smile in his voice. My pissed voice didn't faze him for a second. "I was just asking Lindy if she didn't mind some visitors tomorrow. You know, just the usual crowd."

"No. Not tomorrow, next week."

'But—"

"Next week, Julian, I'm sure you can all wait."

"Fine," he snapped. "Come Monday, your woman is ours."

I snorted. "Today is Sunday, Julian. Make it Wednesday and we have a deal."

"Seriously?"

88

"Yes."

He sighed loud and long, then finally said, "Fine."

Chuckling I said, "Right. Night, Julian."

"Night, spunk-rat."

Shaking my head, I hung up the phone, and sat back turning to Malinda. "You cool with them coming here?"

"Um, yes. I think. They seem like a nice group of people."

"They're crazy, wild and... fuck, just crazy. But they are good people."

She smiled up at me. "Okay, Declan."

Goddamn, I loved that smile, because that smile told me she wanted to get to know my people.

"Love?"

"Yes?"

"Can I ask... are you right for money? I wasn't sure what your situation was. Christ, ah, if you need help with anything, just let me know, yeah?"

She looked up at me with warm eyes. "I'm, um, it's all good. Tank used to give me a weekly allowance. I had some saved and... now that he's gone... he, um, had life insurance. So, I'm good. Thank you though."

Fuck, she was cute. I could tell she was uncomfortable; still she managed to inform me that her bank account was cool.

Hell, even if it wasn't, I would have helped out.

Before I jumped her bones and freaked the kids out if they happened to come out I said, "Get your kids in bed, love. Then you."

For a moment, I swore I saw disappointment, but then it vanished. In its place was a small smile, and for the last time

89

that night, she shocked the hell outta me. She stood from the couch, turned, bent down and touched her lips to mine. "Night, Declan."

I reached up and ran my hand down her cheek. "Night, love."

CHAPTER NINE

MALINDA

*D*amn Declan Stoke and his... amazingness. I'd gone to bed last night as horny as an animal in heat. Maybe I was in heat? *Do women do that?* That kiss, his luscious lips upon mine was divine.

Still, in a way I was thankful Mrs Cliff had interrupted, because if she hadn't, I would have been naked, straddling Stoke on that couch, while my children were in their rooms. That was the worse a mother could do.

He drove my body insane in the most delicious way possible. He also drove my mind insane with how it felt like he knew me.

After Mrs Cliff left, I was about to tell him that it shouldn't have happened. He knew that, which was why he changed the subject, I was glad he did. Because if I had told him I regretted it and wished it hadn't happened, it would have one hundred percent, been a lie.

I was more than glad it happened, which scared me. It made me feel like I had betrayed Tank. However, it made me feel alive. Wanted. Desired.

But there was no denying the chemistry Declan Stoke and I had.

So that night, instead of living my fantasy, I went to bed and played out my own, pretending Declan had snuck into my room to have his wicked way with me. I had never come so hard and long in my life. It made me wonder what the real Declan Stoke would be like—if he'd live up to my fantasy.

I WOKE in the morning relaxed and sated. After my shower, I made my way into the kitchen to find a repeat of the morning after the event. Nary was at the table eating cereal. She waved at me and smiled. Josh stood opposite Stoke over the kitchen bench, and while Stoke leaned against the counter in nothing but jeans, Josh stared up at him while talking and waving wild hands around in the air.

"Morning," I said to everyone in general.

"Hey, Mum. I was just telling Stoke about Death Force, the game I was playing last night while you two were making out on the couch."

Thankfully, I wasn't drinking anything at that time because I was certain I would have choked on it and died.

Stoke burst out a rumble of laughter and I turned my shocked, embarrassed face to Nary, who was giggling.

"I– what... um."

"Mum." Josh rolled his eyes. "Nary and I are cool with it. We're down with Stoke being your boyfriend."

"W-what... why are... huh?"

"After I spotted you and Stoke on the couch last night—" he started chuckling and I k new why with his next words. "Before Mrs Cliff came in, I went and talked to Nary about it. She's fine with it, so this morning, after Stoke woke us up I had a man-to-man talk with him. He knows if he hurts you, we'll hate him."

Oh. My.

"But—" I started only to stop when Stoke started for me.

He walked up, wound an arm around my waist and brought me flush against him. With his other hand, he cupped my jaw and tilted my head up to meet his amused gaze. "You down with this?"

"With what?" I whispered.

"Me bein' your old man?"

"I... I'm not sure. I, um...." I leaned in and uttered into his ear as he moved his hand to my neck, "We only just kissed last night. Well, besides... but...."

I moved my head back in time to see his smile. "Kids. Give us a moment."

"No worries, Stoke," Josh said and bounded out of the room. I saw Nary quietly follow him. She was smiling so wide I was sure she'd crack her jaw.

"Love." I turned to look at him. He gave my neck a

squeeze as he searched my face, then he asked, "Did you play with yourself last night?"

"Stoke," I gasped.

He chuckled. "You did and I bet you did it while thinkin' of me." I didn't answer, but he smiled smugly. "Yep, you did." Another neck squeeze. "And it was good."

A light punch in his stomach had him laughing. "Love, we'll go slow. You're kids are down with me bein' your old man... but will you be?"

"Uh... can I give you an answer tonight?" I asked as my brain screamed at me to say yes, but my damaged heart was singing "Grenade" by Bruno Mars.

He watched me for a few beats and then grinned. "Sure, love." He then touched his lips lightly to mine. He went to pull away, but my body wasn't for that. I reached up, wrapped my arms around his neck and deepened the kiss. His hands moved to my bottom and forced my hips closer to his, close enough I could feel his hardness.

I'm such a hussy! I asked for a day to think and yet I was kissing the hell out of this man. *All that says is I'm a tease.* Dammit, who was I kidding anyway? My answer was going to be yes.

"Yes," I mumbled around his mouth. He stopped kissing me and I let out a disappointed growl.

"What did you just say?" he asked.

"Y-yes?"

His smile was bright. "You're willing to give this a chance?"

I couldn't say it. Instead, it seemed my body was making me out to be the hussy, so it nodded my head for me.

"Don't worry. We'll get to know one another. You'll learn to trust me. I would never hurt you or your kids intentionally."

All I could do was pray he was right. I had been through enough heartache in my thirty-five years, but worse, my children had been through enough to last them a lifetime.

Stoke continued, "We'll leave it—for now—to the same routine. I'll come by every second or third day for dinner and we'll see how it goes, yeah?"

Smiling shakily, I agreed, "Yeah."

"Fuckin' elated you want to try this with me."

There was nothing I could say to that. A thank you didn't seem enough. Declan Stoke was elated to become more of a standard part in my life. I was honoured he picked me. A broken woman, healing slightly every day, who had two children and they had their own daddy issues. But he was willing to take us all on. For that, *I* was elated.

Instead of saying anything, I showed him. I kissed him with so much enthusiasm I was dizzy. He gripped me tightly to him and groaned against my mouth. I smiled; happy I could even draw a groan out of him. I wanted to hear it again and again.

However, in the kitchen with the kids in the next room wasn't the time.

"I guess she's for the idea?" I heard Josh laugh. We pulled back, both panting. With wide eyes, I turned to look at my son, but he wasn't the only one standing there. Dodge, Stoke's biker brother, stood beside him with a wide smile upon his face. He also looked like he was fighting his own laugh.

Stoke turned to the bench away from them, at first I wondered why. Until I remembered a certain firm hardness that had been rubbing against me. He was trying to get himself under control.

"Ah, hi, Dodge." I gave a small wave his way. His smile went wider, which I ignored, but didn't stop my face from heating though. "Josh, I, um, are you ready for school?"

Josh cackled with laughter. "Yeah, Mum." He moved off to the front door.

"You all right, brother, or you need some time?" Dodge taunted.

"I'll meet you at the car," Stoke growled low, that was when Dodge started to laugh. "Just make sure Nary's in the car ready," Stoke snapped.

"She's already out there. Didn't want to see her mum neckin'. Apparently, it's gross. But I didn't mind it one bit."

Next thing I knew, a plastic container flew over my head and hit Dodge in the chest. "Out," Stoke hissed. Dodge walked off chuckling. Declan wrapped me in his arms again and said, "Wish I could make it tonight, finish what we started here but I can't. I guess it's good in a way, because it would have meant going slowly would be out the window."

"That's true." I smiled.

He groaned, kissed me hard and walked out of the house.

NARY

I was standing at my locker at the end of the day smiling to myself. I'd never seen my mum that happy before. Even if Stoke was another biker, like my dad had been, Josh and I knew he was different. For one, he showed up at the house wanting to spend time with us, and two, he showed he cared.

The smile slipped from my mouth. It was sad to lose Dad, but in a way, I was glad, and I hated myself for that thought.

Josh needed a guy around the house and Stoke was perfect for him. I knew I'd put mum through hell recently. Always talking back, but it was because I thought she didn't care. She kept us with a man who hated us, who yelled at us every day. In a way, I understood it, or at least I tried to. She didn't want us to have a broken home. Even if we were all broken already because of the way Dad was.

Josh and I were going to do our best to cause nothing that could take Stoke away from our family.

"Hey, lesbo, had any fingering today?"

I groaned, closed my locker and turned to the person I hated the most. Malcolm French. He was in the same grade as me, year eleven, and he had been an annoying turd since he arrived at our school two years ago.

The only reason he gave me hell was because I said I wouldn't date him. It wasn't because he wasn't good look-ing. He was. But he was mean to most people. He was rude and everything he said was disgusting. He stood leaning against the opposite wall from my locker. He always found time to go out of his way to taunt and tease me.

"Malcolm, just leave me alone." I sighed, picked my bag from the floor and started down the hallway.

Shit.

He followed behind me. Usually he waited until there was an audience to play with my mind, but today, the halls were deserted...except for Saxon Black. My eyes always seemed to find him even if it was crowded. He was tall and in the year above me. He was a bad boy in many ways. Though, I think it had a lot to do with his home life. He looked the part also, charcoal hair, faded jeans with holes in them, black tees with some rock band on them and motorcycle boots. He stood down the hall a bit, with his locker open, but his beautiful green eyes were on Malcolm and me, only they had a look of revulsion within them. That look seemed to be placed on his handsome face a lot when I was around. I never knew why though.

"Stop ignoring me, slut," Malcolm jeered behind me.

"Maybe if I do it long enough, you'll just disappear." I shouldn't have said it. I knew for some time now to keep my mouth shut around Malcolm. But he brought it out in me. Everyone had a right to stick up for themselves. Only when I did it with Malcolm, he hated it and he'd think of a new way to make me pay for it.

"Nary, come on," Josh called from down the hall.

"Fucking lucky he came, lesbo, one day you will pay and I'll be the one to deliver it." Malcolm sneered.

Shrugging his words off like I always did, I made my way to my brother, averting my eyes from Saxon.

CHAPTER TEN

MALINDA

"Well, hello there, Lindy," Julian cried as I opened the door. I shook my head. I hadn't expected Julian—I looked around him—Mattie, Zara, Deanna, Ivy and Clary, until the following day. Yet there they were, standing on the porch.

"Um, sorry, come in. I thought you were the groceries being delivered." Declan didn't want me to go to the super-market so I had to do everything online and get it delivered.

I led them all into the kitchen. "I thought you were all coming tomorrow?" I asked

"We were," Zara started as she sat down at the table. Mattie and Julian opted to sit at on the seats at the bench, while the rest of the ladies and myself, sat around the kitchen table. "But then Julian came up with the idea to annoy Stoke for keeping you to himself, so to speak, so we came a day early." She smiled.

"He hasn't actually been keeping me to himself. I only see him every second day."

"Aw, isn't that cute? She's protecting him already," Julian gushed.

"Cute, yeah, what would be sweeter is if I had a hot chocolate in my hand about now. I was promised treats, dammit," Deanna whined. Without looking at her, Zara pulled a chocolate bar out of her bag and handed it over. Deanna smiled, unwrapped it quickly and started munching. It was as though Zara had calmed the beast.

"We soon realised, now she's pregnant, to carry treats in our bags or she gets cranky real quick," Ivy explained.

I giggled. "I was a sweet tooth when I was pregnant."

"Lindy, we heard Warden has been calling you Mally, which would you prefer?"

Smiling, I said, "Mally."

"Done," he grinned. "Now, as Talon calls us, we muffka-teers need to bring you into our fold. When a girl is down—"

"Maybe I should go. I'm sure I still have my man card," Mattie interrupted.

"Oh, no baby, you stay. You're here for moral support." He patted his partner's knee and continued, "So, when a girl is down, we reach out to one another. When a girl is sick, we reach out. When a girl just needs to rant, we reach out. We even reach out when it's that time of the month and we need a girls' night of Chris Hemsworth and chocolate. What I'm saying, darling Mally, is you are now a part of our fold. You need us for anything, you call us and we will be there."

I'd been with Tank since I was sixteen. I got pregnant at eighteen. I thought he was enough, but I knew I missed something, that something sat in my kitchen reaching out, even though they didn't know me.

It was all too much. I burst into tears. I covered my face with my hands and cried myself silly.

"You made her leak," Deanna yelled. "Oh, shit, I think I'm gonna leak. Bitches, you made me leak." Her outrage actually made me feel better. Wiping my eyes, I looked to Deanna to see her throw her chocolate down and rub her eyes.

That was when the back door opened and Dodge came running in, only to come to an abrupt halt and puff out, "I couldn't stop her. She had my balls in a death grip."

"Malinda," Mrs Cliff yelled. "I don't care if it's my fault that guy can't have kids now, he shouldn't fucking stop me from coming in. Tell him, Malinda, I can come and go as I please." She stopped when she spotted everyone and then turned to me and glared. "You're having a fucking party and you didn't invite me. Jesus Christ, girl. My heart just shattered. Fuck it, I'm here now. I'm over it. Now, what are we eating?"

That was why I loved Mrs Cliff. She'd beat anyone to a pulp, tell you how it was, and if something upset her, she'd get over it. Really, she was the crazy, lovable mother I never had.

Julian gasped. "Wow, oh, wow. Hell Mouth, I think we just found your granny."

Clary and Ivy started giggling when Zara said, "It's like looking in a mirror."

What silenced the room was when both Deanna and Mrs Cliff spoke at the same time.

"Fuck off, bitch, I ain't old and haggy."

"Fuck off, girl, I ain't young and slutty." Mrs Cliff smiled. "I think I'll like you."

Deanna rolled her eyes. Still, no one missed the smile playing on her lips. "Yeah, I suppose you could be okay."

"Fuck this shit," Dodge growled, then disappeared out the back door.

Mrs Cliff took the quiet moment to walk around and sit at the end of the table. "Now, what are we talking about? Sex?"

Rolling my eyes, I answered, "No."

"But we should," came from Deanna. "Have you done the dirty with Stoke?"

My eyes widened.

"Wait," Julian yelled. "We need coffee and cake for this. Mattie, honey, I brought a cake with us. It's in the car. Can you go get it while I get the kettle on."

"Bloody lucky I popped in for this talk." Mrs Cliff smiled.

"We aren't talking about sex," I stated.

Ivy, who was sitting next to me at the table, touched my arm gently and said, "Just go with it. If they don't hear it from you, they'll go to Stoke. Besides, they like to talk about everything."

"But—"

"However," Clary began, "we do know to keep it to

ourselves."

"She's right, Mally. What is said in the posse stays in the posse," Julian confirmed.

Looking down at the table, I admitted, "I'm not used to this. I haven't had friends most of my life."

"It can be overwhelming. Believe me I know," Clary said. "I was the same; except I had a sister"

Deanna scoffed, "A bitch sister."

"Yes, that's true." She grimaced. "Mally, we each have a story to tell. I was blind in a lot of ways until I met Blue and our posse." She grinned. "I know now, I wouldn't change it for anything. Deanna can be a bitch and swear like a trooper, but she also has a sweet side and would do anything for you—"

"I do not," Deanna snapped.

"Ivy may chat a lot, but she means well by it and we love her for it. Zara is the ringleader. She is fiercely protective and can seem a little crazy, but she's beautifully natured." She paused and looked to Julian with soft eyes. "Julian… he's amazing. He's loyal, funny, gorgeous, calm and he's the glue that keeps us all together. What also has us stuck, is that we're all willing to take hold and help each other out. With time, you'll need it if you're going to be a part of Stoke's life. Those biker boys are…"

"Hot-headed, arrogant, possessive, alpha males." Zara smiled. "I've had practise with that one."

We all laughed.

"You'll need us to understand them and bitch when they do or say the wrong thing, which will happen a lot," Clary said.

"Can we get over this sappy shit now and get down to the dirty deets?" Deanna asked.

Mrs Cliff slammed her hand down onto the table and yelled, "I like you. You're fucking adopted."

"Aw shit, old lady. Now *you're* going to make me leak," Deanna snapped in response.

"Mrs Cliff, Deanna's pregnant. She's highly emotional right now," Zara offered.

"You got knocked up? I hope it was by a hot guy."

"Oh, yeah." Deanna grinned.

"I'd like to meet my new grandson-in-law. Dinner my house tonight."

"I'm down with that."

Oh. My.

Poor Griz was walking into Hell on Earth and he didn't know it yet. I wondered if he'd even heard of her.

The front door opened, in came Mattie, carrying a plastic bag filled with goodies, and Griz, who stood just inside the open doorway glaring at his wife.

"Woman," he barked. "You've got an appointment. What the fuck are you doin' here?"

"Don't you 'woman' me," Deanna snapped and stood from the table with her hands on her hips. "I wasn't missing out on the hot gossip of how good Stoke is in bed. We can re-schedule."

"You ain't missin' it. I'm sure your women can fill you in," he growled low.

"Fine," she growled back. "Besides, we're comin' back here tonight after we get Swan."

"What the fuck for?"

"We're having dinner at Mrs Cliff's," Deanna stated and I swear all colour faded from the big guy's face. He searched the table and found Mrs Cliff smiling at him.

He rolled his eyes and announced, "We aren't comin'."

Uh. Oh.

Mrs Cliff's smile fell from her face and she glared at Griz. "You will be fucking coming, even if I have to come after you and drag you to my house. I don't take a liking to many people and I took one to your lady. You, I'm not so sure. But if you want your lady's adopted nanna in her life, you had bloody better work on winning me over."

Griz's eyes snapped to his wife. "Adopted?"

"What can I say? I'm fucking lovable." She grinned.

I was sure everyone could read the murderous look on Griz's face. Deanna was going to have to make things up to him and in a big way.

"We're leavin'," he snarled.

"Sure thing, babe." She moved around the table to her man.

"See you tonight," Mrs Cliff called.

I wasn't sure, but I think Griz confirmed they'd be there with a lot of rough words and swearing.

"How far along is she?" I asked Zara.

"Just about three months. The wench kept it a secret for two months."

So she was past the scary stage. I wasn't sure I could imagine seeing Deanna as a mother. Until Zara next informed me of Swan, Griz's three year old.

Julian passed out the coffee and cake as Zara informed me of her story. I was shocked she had been through so much, but happy that she had Talon while going through it all.

"Those bikers are hot motherfuckers," Mrs Cliff announced after Ivy told us all her story. "Now, I want to hear how your biker's holding up in the sack?" she asked me.

Blushing, I said, "Um, we haven't actually slept with each other."

Ivy and Clary gasped. Julian's spoon with cake on it clattered to the table. Mattie rolled his eyes and Zara stared at me with wide eyes.

"That can't be," Julian said his hand going to his heart. "How long has he been around? Three weeks? I thought for sure he would have made his move."

"We've kissed," I offered. "But it was only yesterday that I said yes to being...his woman." The words felt foreign as they passed my lips, but as soon as it hit my ears, an ease and rightness settled over me.

"He's a good kisser," Mrs Cliff said and all eyes turned to her. "Oh, don't look at me like that. It ain't like I pashed the shit out of him. Though, I wouldn't mind trying." I opened my mouth to say something, but she got there first. "Kidding, child. However, I have seen them make out and it was H.O.T." She actually spelled out the words like a dorky teenager, making the heat sitting on my cheeks inflame even more.

"Well, at least it's something," Julian said and resumed eating his cake.

"You really need to stop getting off on other people's sex lives," Mattie sighed, but his smile told me he didn't care at all.

"He's coming for dinner tonight," I said.

The women grinned and Julian clapped his hands together. "I've got it. You need to seduce him. Wear something sexy and when he climbs into bed—"

"He sleeps on the couch," I interrupted.

Julian gasped. "Oh, my God, he what?"

"Like I said, we haven't been... doing this long. So when he stays, he sleeps on the couch. It's like he doesn't want to risk rushing things."

Clary groaned. "Oh, I know how that feels."

"Do you want him?" Mrs Cliff asked.

Blushing harder, which was no small feat since I was sure my cheeks were already the brightest they could be, I said, "I, um, I think so."

"Dose he make your heart rush when you see him?" Zara asked.

"Do you get all tingly when he walks into the room?" Ivy asked with a small smile.

"Does your vagina sing when you spot him?" Mrs Cliff asked.

"Mrs Cliff," I snapped.

"It's like Deanna hasn't even left," Mattie said, shaking his head.

"So?" Julian asked.

I forced myself not to lower my head as I spoke, even though I wanted to crawl in some sort of hole with my embarrassment. "All of those and more."

"Hoo-boy," Julian cackled.

"Don't worry," Ivy said. "All our men do that for us."

The talking, sharing was perplexing. It was awkward in more ways than one, but when we all burst out laughing, it was special. Call me crazy, but I liked our girl talk.

It was then we all turned in our seats to the front door as we heard tires squealing out the front. I stood, my hand going to my neck as the front door flung open. Through it first was a scared-looking Josh. Next came a boy I'd never seen before, after that was Stoke; he carried a crying Nary in his arms.

"Nary," I gasped and ran to her.

Stoke sat her down on the couch. I quickly placed myself next to her and brought her head to my chest as she shook and sobbed.

"What happened?" I demanded with my jaw clenched. I wanted to hurt the person responsible for my daughter being distraught.

"She was attacked at school," Stoke growled.

"O-Oscar?" I asked.

"No, some fuckin' little shit who's about to get more than the beating this kid gave him," Stoke explained and pointed to the boy I hadn't seen before. Stoke then bent, kissed Nary's forehead and whispered, "Everything will be good, girl."

I felt Nary nod against my chest. Stoke pulled back a little and gave me a swift kiss on the lips. "I may be late for dinner. I got some shit to deal with. Saxon, get in the car," her ordered the boy, straight away that child listened.

I nodded to Stoke, my mind reeling. Turning to Clary, I gestured for her to take Nary. Once I moved out of the way, Clary sat down next to my daughter and cradled her. I walked Stoke out the front door, and onto the porch. I turned to him and took a step closer, gripping his tee I asked, "Did he…."

His hands went to my arms. "No, it was fuckin' close, love, but no. She's gonna have bruises tomorrow though."

"Where is he?" I snapped.

"In the car with Dive, Blue and Billy."

"What are you going to do?"

"I'm takin' him home and gonna have a nice chat to his 'rents."

"Before… before you do that, make him pay."

Stoke's eyes widened, then he smiled. "I'd love to do that for you, love, but he's in a heap of pain already from Saxon. He found them and beat the shit outta him. I'll just make sure he never does it again."

"Okay, handsome."

"Fuckin' love that," he growled, then said, "I'm heading to Saxon's place after that. He's got a shit dad. I wanna talk to him." He smiled, I knew Saxon's dad wasn't going to like that talk. "If things don't go well, I need you to make up that single bed in Josh's room. He'll be sleeping here tonight."

With a nod, I said, "Of course. Be safe, Declan."

"I will. Also tonight, I'm sleeping in your bed."

"Okay," I agreed straight away and he smiled big.

"Get back to your girl. She's gonna need you."

"Okay, handsome." Kissing him quickly, I stepped back. Before he took off, I sent a wave his way. He shook his head smilin' and gave me a chin lift.

I turned around and went to my girl.

CHAPTER ELEVEN

ONE HOUR EARLIER

NARY

I was walking from the cafeteria to my locker before the bell rang to grab my PE clothes. Once I'd collected my things, I arrived early to PE. I headed into the changing rooms to get into my kit, hoping I'd have time to get to a new level on Angry Birds on my phone.

My head was full of other thoughts, which was why I didn't hear the door behind me open just after I walked in. I didn't hear anything.

But I felt something. Shoved hard in the back, I fell to the floor on my knees. I cried out in pain, and move to my bottom to see who had done it. Looking up, I saw Malcolm leering down at me. His eyes full of hatred.

"W-what are you doing in here?"

"I'm sick of your shit, lesbo. You think you're so much better than me—"

"I don't," I cried out. "I never have."

"Bullshit," he screamed down at me. "I've seen them."

"Who?"

"Those men who drop you off and pick you up. You're a little slut after all, yet you can't even give it to me."

I didn't see it coming. His booted foot connected with my ribs. I collapsed to my side and screamed in pain.

"Well, I think it's my turn," he sneered, then bent over, gripped my ankle and dragged me over the cold tiled floor. I kicked at him with my other leg, but he ignored it. I couldn't aim for the most vital part because he was turned away from me. With my hands, I tried to keep my skirt down, but as he dragged me, it kept riding up.

I wished I'd had the chance to get changed into my PE clothes, the shorts and tee. He dragged me deeper into the changing rooms. I screamed, yelled and swore for help.

Where was everyone?

Tears blurred my vision; still, I knew never to give up.

I wouldn't, couldn't let it happen.

He flung my leg to the ground and stepped back. Looking down at me, he laughed. "You look pathetic. For once, you don't look like the cool, calm, Nary May. The girl with a fit figure, long hair and perfect green eyes. Now you look like you come from the streets. Which I suppose is appropriate, seems you hooker yourself out to all those guys," he jeered.

I scrambled up to and crab walked backward away from him, screaming over and over, "Leave me alone. Leave me *alone.*"

He followed my attempts of escape and smiled smugly down at me. "Enough of these games," he said with a punch to my face. My head whipped sideways and I cried out in agony. While I was still dazed from the blow, he got to his knees and with forceful hands, he pushed my legs apart.

"No, no, no," I screamed, sitting up to push at his chest as he tried to lay down on top of me. I shoved, punched and yelled.

That was when I saw it.

Out the corner of my eye, a shadow at the end of the lockers.

It wasn't there for long, soon disappearing.

"Help, please," I begged to whomever that shadow belonged to.

"Shut up, slut," Malcolm hissed and hit me in the stomach, hard enough to leave me gasping for breath. I fell back to the tiled floor, my hands going to my stomach, my back arching as I fought for air.

I couldn't do anything, other than cry and plead.

I wanted to die.

Malcolm had gripped my panties and roughly jerked at them, my body moved with the vicious moves.

That when I heard a tear and a thump.

Then everything went deathly silent.

Until it all came rushing back in. I scrambled my sore

body up to my elbows to see Saxon on top of Malcolm, punching him over and over, to any undefended place on his body. Malcolm's hands were up over his face, protecting himself. Still, when Saxon hit Malcolm in the side, his hands fell away and Saxon went to town. His lips split in seconds. He had a cut above his eyebrow next.

I knew I should have stopped him. I didn't want Saxon in trouble for helping me.

But I didn't.

I couldn't.

Instead, I sat frozen as I watched Saxon deliver more pain to Malcolm than I had ever seen.

A flurry of noises and voices hit me next. I looked up in time to see a livid Stoke barrelling toward us.

STOKE

I was sitting in my black pick-up in the school carpark with a brother named Dive, because he liked to dive onto women's pussies, just shooting the shit when Dive uttered, "What the fuck?" and shot out of the car.

I was on my feet beside the car in seconds, what I saw sent ice through my veins. Josh was running like Hell was on his heels toward us. Both Dive and I started forward just as fast.

My hands landed on his shoulders as I barked, "What the fuck, kid?"

He puffed and panted out, "Nary... in... trouble... changing rooms."

Without looking at Dive—I knew he would follow—we all headed into the school. The halls were bustling with people. I could feel eyes on us as we pushed past so many students, with Josh leading the way. "Call Blue and Billy. They're on backup today," I said over my shoulder.

I knew without a doubt, he would do as I asked. I was ready to kick some arse and I'd need backup, not only to hold me back if Nary was hurt, but to keep the other vultures at bay.

As we rounded a corner, I could see the sign to the changing rooms. I grabbed Josh by the shoulder and ordered, "Stay out here." I looked to Dive; he gave me a chin lift, understanding what I was asking. He was to keep Josh outta the room no matter what they heard. A bell chimed throughout the school.

"Nary has PE. A heap of other students are heading this way for it too," Josh said as he rubbed his chest. He'd run like a fucking champion.

"How long 'til backup?"

"'Bout five," Dive answered.

"'Til then, keep anyone who comes by out," I ordered and then started for the door. Just before I entered, I pulled my gun from the back of my jeans and slid the door open quietly.

After the door closed behind me, I heard it.

Grunted moans filled with pain.

Forgetting the stealth and wanting to catch whatever the

fuck was going down, I ran toward the sounds. My booted feet slapped hard against the tiled floor.

Coming around a corner, I stopped dead.

Nary was sitting in a corner, her hands behind her, obviously supporting her weight. She stared on with a look of terror, yet awe in front of her. Some guy was sitting on another, laying punch after punch into the dude on the ground.

Before it led to death and Nary witnessing it, I stalked over, grabbed the kid off the other and hauled him up to stand next to me. He went to go for the kid on the ground again, but with a hand across his chest, I brought him back against me and growled, "Enough."

"Stoke," Nary uttered on a sob.

"Tell me what the fuck is goin' on so we can get outta here," I barked.

"Let go of me, man," the guy I got pinned by the chest growled.

"You cool?" I asked

"Yeah,"

Removing my arm, I took a step back and ordered, "Talk."

I was expecting the words to come from Nary, but they didn't. The dude who was beating the shit outta the other guy did. "I saw Nary leave the cafeteria early and when I spotted the dickhead, Malcolm, on her tail, I knew he was up to something. So I followed. When he went into the girls' changing room after Nary, I knew it wasn't gonna be good. I found Josh as fast as I could and told him to get you guys. I hurried back here… but, I wasn't fast enough." With that, he landed a kick into the Malcolm's side. "He'd already laid his hands on her and kicked her. Fuck…." He whirled away from Malcolm, though I could see he didn't want to. He wanted to finish the job he started. "He was gonna rape her, man."

"What?" I hissed. "Nary, this true, girl?"

She said nothing, but after a beat, she nodded.

Kneeling down next to the quiet Malcolm, I got real close. He averted his eyes from me, so I grabbed his jaw hard and turned his face to mine. "Do you know who I am?" I snarled in his face.

He studied me for a moment, then hissed, "No."

Smiling without humour, I said, "You just fucked-up big time. Have you heard of Hawks Motorcycle club?" The guy's eyes widened. Yeah, he'd heard of us. "I'm a member and I'm datin' her mum. Meaning she's part of Hawks. When people fuck with Hawks, we fuck back… big time."

The guy's face was bathed in blood. I wished I had been the one to deliver it, but from the wet patch on the front of his pants, I got satisfaction enough from scaring him.

"Stoke?" Blue called from the front.

Standing, I answered with, "Back here." I looked to the guy who delivered payback for Nary. "Your name?"

"Saxon Black."

I eyed him for a bit, then asked, "He give you that black eye?"

"No," he hissed with a raised upper lip.

"Who?"

Before he answered, Blue came around the corner and whistled low. "What do we have here?"

I pointed a finger to the fucker on the ground. "Take him outta here the best way no one will see. He touched my woman's girl, even though Saxon here dealt enough payback, I wanna make sure he never does it again."

"There's a side door that way. It leads out to the courtyard," Saxon explained. "Just don't go that way," he pointed in a different direction. "The PE teacher will be there or she could be headin' in here soon to see what the delay is."

"Right," Blue said. With a look of disgust aimed at Malcolm, he strode over, yanked him up and over his shoulder.

"Saxon, as soon as Blue is out, go tell the others at the door we're ready to roll."

He said nothing. With watchful eyes, he waited until Blue disappeared around the corner. He took one glance at Nary and said, "Sorry I was late." Then left to do as I said.

I approached Nary with caution. I was worried she'd freak out with a male so close after what she'd just went through. However, I shouldn't have worried. As soon as I crouched down next to her, she flung herself into my arms. She wrapped her arms around my neck tightly and cried into my neck. I picked her up and started for the side door. "Let's get you home to your mum, yeah?" I felt her nod against my neck. "Everythin' will be fine, Nary. You got that, right?"

"Yes, Stoke," she whispered.

We reached my truck. Josh was sitting in the back with the door open waiting for his sister. As soon as I deposited her in there, he took her hand in his. I closed the door and wished I could beat the little shit again for what he did to make Nary hunch into herself.

Hopping in the driver seat, I looked to Saxon beside me and gave him a chin life. "We're dropping off Nary and Josh first. Then we're goin' to see that fucker's 'rents. But now, I wanna know who gave you that black eye?" I started the car and looked to the vehicle behind me. Billy, Blue and Dive were in there with the little shit. I smiled at the thought of the crap they'd be scaring him with.

Turning my attention back to a silent Saxon, who was sitting there glaring out the windscreen, I said, "Kid, just fuckin' tell me."

"It ain't any of your Goddamn business," he snapped.

"Look at me," I hissed. Once I had his eyes, I explained, "You helped out Hawks today. We repay that favour, I'm guessin', this shit happens to you a lot. I also reckon it's a family issue. But it's one I can help put a stop to."

He snorted. "I doubt it."

"Give me a try," I said and manoeuvred the car out of the carpark.

"My father," he uttered, his upper lip rose. It was just what I had thought.

AFTER WE DROPPED off Josh and Nary, and after my woman gave me a fuckin' hard-on from the way she talked, wantin' to deliver pain to the guy who harmed her daughter. I got back in the pick-up with Saxon and followed Blue's vehicle to Malcolm's house. Of-fuckin'-course it had to be in the middle of fuckin' toffy area.

When we pulled up out the front I told Saxon to wait in the car. I climbed out, walked around my truck and waited on the walkway as Blue and Dive got a sore lookin' Malcolm outta the car.

"He fuckin' pissed himself again. You're cleaning my goddamn car, Stoke," Blue complained.

"Who made him piss himself?" I asked as we headed up the walkway to his triple-story brick home.

"Billy," Dive supplied.

"Serious?" I asked, bloody surprised it had been the youngest member.

"Yep," Blue smiled. It was obvious he was proud. "Told this arsehole that if he fought what was gonna go down, he was gonna turn up at his house in the middle of the night, crawl into his bed, where he would first cut out his tongue, so he couldn't scream, and then he'd rape him with his hunting knife."

I whistled. "That'd do the trick."

"Beautiful moment, if it wasn't for the piss now staining my fuckin' seat."

We walked onto the porch and I rang the bell. "Then Billy has to clean it, not me. He's the one who made him piss himself."

"Y-you will all pay for this," Malcolm said.

We looked at each other and burst out laughing. I highly doubted we would because I was pretty sure I knew who his father was.

As soon as an old, short, fat bald guy opened the door and screamed in fright, I knew I'd been right.

"Afternoon, Peter."

"What did you do to my son?" he yelled.

"Now, now, Peter, you need to keep your voice down," Dive said.

We all knew who Peter French was. He was a regular in boss's strip clubs. In fact, he was in them nearly every night. Talon made sure to know, in detail, who his regulars were. We all knew Peter was an investment banker who stole money from his clients to live in his nice house and be married to Kathy, the local gold diggin' whore. It was obvious Malcolm wasn't Kathy's child, since she was only twenty and Malcolm was the same age as Nary.

I took a step forward and got in Peter's face. When he saw I wasn't happy, he paled. "You need to listen and make sure you take it all in. I highly suggest you ship your son off to the Army Reserves. He needs to learn some fuckin' manners."

"What did he do to earn Hawks attention?" Peter asked.

"He touched a member of ours—"

"She isn't a fuckin' member," Malcolm shouted. Dive took the opportunity to shut him up by a light touch to his stomach.

I turned to him. "That's where you are wrong, kid. Like I said, I'm datin' her mum. She's my woman and when that happens, her and her kids become mine. Meaning they become a part of Hawks." I went back to Peter. "Get him out of town. I don't wanna see him for a very fuckin' long time. If your son steps into this town without us knowing about it first, he will be dead." Peter spluttered and was about to spew some shit, but I got in his face. "He had his hands on my woman's girl. He kicked her, beat her and was about to rape her. Now I have every right to take his life for what he's already done. However, I won't. He got taught a lesson today by someone. Now, it's your turn to take care of the rest, get him outta here. But don't ever fuckin' forget...no matter where he is, Hawks will be watching. If he steps outta line again, if he tries this shit again or even fuckin' looks at a woman the wrong way... he will be dealt with, and you know what that means, Peter."

"If I don't?" he stupidly questioned.

"Then Kathy will know where you go every night, and your clients will be receiving an email about the shit you have been doing to them for years. Fuck, we may just do that anyway because of the shit your son's done." I stood straight and smiled viciously. "So watch yourself, Peter French."

With that, I turned my back on him, and sent a chin lift to Blue and Dive. They shoved Malcolm forward. Peter being the dumb fuck he was, wasn't ready for it, so Malcolm went sailing to the floor in a heap, crying out in pain.

Before I reached my pick-up, I said to my brothers, "I've got one more thing to deal with." I gestured with my head to the waiting Saxon.

"Do you want backup?" Blue asked.

"Not sure I'd need it."

"Just in case, brother, I'll go," Dive said.

"Right, I'll take Billy to clean my car before I go collect Clary from your place."

"Thanks for the help today," I said and walked around the car while Dive got into the back.

"Anytime, brother, you know that," Blue called back.

One chin lift later, I climbed in the car and asked Saxon, "Your address?"

"Are you gonna make my dad look like that dude?" Saxon asked.

"Wha'da you mean?" I asked as I started the car.

"That idiot looked like he was gonna throw up, have a heart attack and shit himself all rolled into one."

I shrugged. "I guess we'll see."

Dive chuckled from the back.

CHAPTER TWELVE

STOKE

*U*nlocking the front door to Malinda's house, I was more than ready to crash. That was until I found my dick eager for some attention once he heard the taps in her adjoining bathroom running.

Still, as excited as he was, I stopped in the hallway and first stuck my head in Josh's room. He was sound asleep on his back, arms spread wide, snoring his head off. Across the hall, I opened Nary's door and wasn't surprised to see her laying on her bed with her headphones in, listening to music on her iPod.

My dick shrivelled, knowing that the action was put on hold until I reassured my woman's girl. I walked into the room and watched her slowly sit up and pull the earpieces out.

"You had meds?" I asked, sitting down at the end of her bed.

"Yeah," she said.

"You'll be hurting tomorrow so you'll stay home."

"Okay, Stoke."

I studied her for a moment. She was biting her lower lip, averting her eyes from me and running her hands together. She was fucking stressing over the whole event, I couldn't blame her. Anyone would. "He won't bother you again."

She raised her brows at me.

"He's moving away for a while. You won't see him again, Nary."

Her whole body sagged in relief. She licked her parched lips and asked, "Saxon?"

Fuck me.

Anyone could read into that one question and know that Nary was interested in Saxon.

I'd have to keep an eye on them.

"He's fine. He's at the compound." She bit her bottom lip and then asked, "Why's he there?"

"After we saw his dad, my boss called. Talon, who's the president of Hawks, I told him what went down. He wanted Saxon at the compound in case his dad wasn't smart and wanted to cause some shit for him." I took a breath and laid my hand on her ankle. She flinched but I kept my hand there. "Girl, for what he did for you… it showed us a lotta things about that kid. We asked him if he wanted in the club."

"And?" she asked eagerly.

"He'll be patched in tomorrow as a prospect."

That was when she smiled.

Fuck me.

She was more than keen on Saxon.

"You good for the night now?" I asked.

"Yeah, Stoke." I stood from her bed and headed to the door. I had it all the way open when she called, "Stoke?"

I turned to her and said, "Yeah, sweetheart?"

"Thank you… for, um—"

"Don't mention it. Get some sleep, Nary."

"I will… well, now." She smiled.

I closed the door to her room after I spotted her put her earphones back in and started down the hall again.

Jesus. Seriously?

I looked down at my dick, and felt, more than saw I was hard again.

It was as if he knew I was headed to Malinda's room or he was just pointing the fucking way. Probably scared I'd get lost.

Opening her door, I saw she wasn't in it. I stepped in, closed the door and then looked to the bathroom door that was shut tightly. I could faintly hear soft music drifting from there. A smile lit my face and I was fucking super glad the kids' rooms where a long hallway away and we had a laundry and a bathroom separating our rooms.

Because I was more than ready to take my woman and make her truly mine.

Gripping the bottom of my tee, I pulled it up over my head. Discarding my boots and socks, I walked to the bathroom door in my jeans only. Malinda jumped, letting out a squeak and tried to cover her big boobs with her hands. The rest of her body was already covered by the mountain of bubbles.

"St-Declan, what are you doing in here?" she asked with wide eyes.

"I'm beat, love. I came to see you before I crashed."

She sat up a little and said, "Oh." I bit back my smirk when she sounded deflated. "Yes, um, how did it go?"

"Good," I said and took the couple of steps in to the side of the large bath, where I knelt beside it. I placed my hands on the side and added, "Nary won't have any trouble from that kid anymore. He's leaving town tomorrow. His dad is shipping him off to the Army Reserves. If he doesn't, then his life belongs to Hawks', and we'll do what we should have done for touchin' Nary in the first place."

"No… you, ah, you're doing the right thing," she said distractedly as her eyes roamed my body.

"We'll keep an eye on the little shit. Make sure he doesn't do anything like this again to another girl. If he does, his life will be snuffed out."

She licked her lips and said, "Okay."

"Malinda?" I growled.

Her eyes shot to my face. "Yes?"

"I just told you we'll take a life and you're okay with that?"

Her brows bunched down as if she was confused. "Well… yes. Declan, that boy was going to rape my child. He already beat her and kicked her with such force to have left bruises on her skin. I would have preferred to beat the shit out of him myself, but Nary assured me Saxon dealt with him and he was a bloody mess in the end. Still, if he tries something like this again, then it would be obvious he has a problem. One, I doubt, would be helped with medication. So… if it was to save other women's lives, then one abusive arsehole's life wouldn't matter if someone in the Hawks ended it for him."

Hell. She had just blown my mind and I was about to blow my load.

There she sat in a bubble bath telling me she didn't care if he was taken out by anyone if it saved other people's lives.

She was made for me.

"Declan?" she asked. I could see she was unsure of her little speech.

"Give me your hand, love." She was hesitant. Her arms were still across her breasts, like she was ashamed to let me see her. "Malinda," I growled. She sighed and removed one arm, the closest one to me. Placing it out toward me, I grabbed her wrist and gently tugged. She gasped, and using her other hand, she braced as her whole body moved to the side of the bath. I smiled smugly down at her, because now I could see her gorgeous big breasts bobbing above the water.

She went to quickly move her arm back, the one I wasn't holding but I said, "You cover those beauties again, I'll get pissed." She eyed me to see if I was serious and I was most fuckin' certainly serious. To prove it, I leaned over the bath and slowly sucked one nipple into my mouth. As soon as I had it between my teeth, I bit down and she moaned.

While I paid attention to each breast and she was occupied, her head was back against the bath, her eyes closed and she was left feeling what my mouth, teeth and tongue were doing to her hardened nipples. I slowly slid the zipper on my jeans down and undid the top button, pulling my cock free.

I drew my mouth away from her breast, glided my tongue up her chest then onto her neck and bit down. She moaned and cried out my name. I fucking loved hearing it fall from her sweet mouth. It was then I whispered in her ear, "I gotta feel your hand on me, love." I took her hand, which was still hanging over the bath, and led it to my hard cock. Without hesitation, her small hand wound around my stiffness and slid up and down before my mouth claimed her.

Her eager hand ran up and down my dick with fast movements. She liked what she was doing to me, but fuck, I loved it more.

"Declan," she moaned around my mouth.

"Hang on, love," I said and dipped my hand and arm into the warm bath water, straight between her legs. I took hold of her thigh. She mewed a little, wanting more, her grip tightened on my cock, drawing a groan from me. I slid my hand up and glided two fingers over her bare pussy.

Leaning back just a little, I watched her hand on me as she tugged me off. I caught her lick her lips and then bit down on her bottom one. I ran my fingers down to her core and into her tight little pussy, she opened her mouth, only no sound came out. I watched her chest rise and fall rapidly.

She liked me touching her as well.

"Declan, oh, God. More," she ordered. I arched my fingers inside of her, hitting her sweet spot as my thumb ran over her clit. "Yes," she sighed.

"You like my fingers fuckin' your pussy, love?"

"Yes, God, yes," she moaned.

"Christ, Malinda, you are fuckin' amazin'," I hissed and started to pump my hips forward. My dick slid in and out of her hand faster and faster. My balls tightened. I was close, but I wanted my woman to finish first.

As she spread her legs wider, as wide as the bath would allow, I deepened my fingers and fucked her with more speed and my thumb circled her clit faster.

"I-I'm close," she gasped.

She opened her mouth to cry out, but I slammed my mouth down on hers and swallowed her cries as her pussy's wall clamped down around my two fingers. All the while, her hand didn't let up and loosen around my cock, and I was fucking glad, because in the next second, I squirted my load over the bath wall and floor, grunting through it while I kissed her.

"Fuck," I uttered. I was more than exhausted now. "Come on, love. Get dry and get your arse into bed."

She giggled, a blush lighting her cheeks. "So bossy after you come."

"Damn right, especially after I come so hard from just my woman's touch." I smiled and stood from the floor. Her blush deepened when she saw my drained cock was still out and ready for viewing. I swivelled my hips, shaking my cock at her and added, "See what you did. You tuckered him out."

She burst out laughing. As I slid my jeans off, I leaned over and kissed her, then ordered again, "Get out, woman. I need sleep."

"Um… I would if my legs could walk, but right now, that isn't possible."

Chuckling, I said, "Good to know I tired my woman out then. Imagine what it'll be like after we actually fuck."

"I may need a wheelchair." She grinned.

Snorting, I smiled widely and helped her from the bath. Wrapping a towel around her, I picked her up and carried her to the bed. I placed her on her feet long enough to fling back the covers, before I picked her back up to throw her down. She laughed as her body bounced. I gripped the towel and tugged it from her body. She landed on her stomach and I groaned.

"Christ," I swore, she looked over her shoulder. "Your arse is every man's dream." Reaching out, I slapped it. She gasped and I grinned as a red mark quickly rose on her pale skin. "Jesus, now look what you've done," I growled, standing back up. When she spotted my hard cock, she laughed. Instead of giving my dick what it wanted, I climbed into bed, rolled her over to her side and brought her back against my chest. My dick was nuzzling itself between her arse cheeks. "I think he likes you."

She snorted and then giggled. "That's okay. I think I like him too."

"Good," I growled, then asked, "You know you're not allowed to like anyone else's right? If you did, I'd have to kill him."

I felt her shake her head, but when she spoke, I could tell there was humour in her voice. "As long as he knows the same goes for him."

Thrusting up, I said, "Oh, yeah, he knows, and wouldn't want to go anywhere else."

We settled in and I hoped to Christ my cock got the message that it was sleep time soon.

"Declan?"

"Hmm?"

"Is, um, could... is Saxon here and could he have heard us in the bathroom?"

Hell, I was surprised my woman was shy after what we'd just done; she wasn't during it. Too cute.

I smiled and kissed her neck. "No, love. He ain't here and I checked the kids before I came in. Josh is sound asleep and Nary was listening to music."

She sighed loudly. I chuckled. "Don't you laugh at me," she snapped and hit my thigh. My dick perked up thinking she was ready to play. "But... is he okay?"

I gave her a squeeze around the waist. "Yeah, Malinda. He's all good. Just stayin' at the compound in case his father gives him more shit."

Which wouldn't surprise me. We'd showed to Saxon's rundown, beat-up house, broken windows and all. After we climbed outta the car, his dad was already waiting on the front stoop, with his arms crossed, a frown and a glare directed at his son.

"What shit have you done now, boy?" he yelled.

"Nothin'," Saxon said.

We stopped just in front of him and let him eye us. I didn't have my cut on, but Dive did and once he saw we were a part of Hawks, his eyes narrowed even further.

"You tellin' stories?" he demanded from his son. "Got some balls bringin' Hawks members here, son."

"I didn't bring them. They wanted to come," Saxon said.

It was obvious he'd had enough and was embarrassed by his dad, he walked up the stairs and got just past his a father before he received a fist to the back of the head.

"Bullshit," his dad yelled.

Saxon stumbled forward, his hands going to his head to protect himself. But he didn't need to. His idiot dad went for him again, stupid fuck either forgot we were there, or was dumb enough to think we'd do nothing about it.

Dive grabbed him in a headlock and I sent a hit to his stomach. He groaned and spat to the ground. "Let him up," I ordered. Dive let go of the prick only to grab hold of his arms. I got close and said, "We're takin' your son with us." I looked to a wide-eyed Saxon just in the doorway. "Go, grab all your shit, kid, you ain't comin' back."

"You can't take him," he yelled and struggled from Dive. Only Dive was a huge arse guy and strong as a fucking ox, so he didn't let go.

"Saxon, go," I growled. As soon as he was out of earshot, I pulled a knife from the back of my jeans and put it to dick-head's neck. "You contact him, come near him, or lay one fuckin' finger on that kid again, I will shove this straight up," I dug the tip of the blade into the man's chin, "when they find your dead body, they'll be able to see the blade through your mouth and in the back of your eyes. Do you get me?"

"W-why him?" he asked.

"He saved a Hawks member. We owe him, by owing him, we're taking him away from a motherfucker like you who likes to beat on kids. He's under our protection. You fuck with him, it means you fuck with Hawks. Do I need to explain what that means?"

"A blade to me."

I smirked. "I guess you're not as dumb as you look." I gestured to Dive to let him go. I stood back a step, then planted my fist on the fucker's jaw. "That's for takin' your shit life out on him," I barked.

"I'll go help the kid," Dive said while grinnin' like a fool.

"You do that." As Dive and Saxon loaded up the car, I stood guard over his father. He was smart once again and said nothing to his son.

My woman's words brought me back into the bedroom. "So Talon doesn't mind Saxon staying there?"

"Nah, love. I rang Talon after we'd been to his house and told him what went down, said I was bringing the kid to the compound. He was all for it, suggested the kid be patched in for what he did for Nary."

"Wow."

I chuckled. "Yeah, Malinda, wow."

"I must make some cookies for him."

What was it with women baking cookies?

"Who?" I questioned.

"Saxon."

"That's all right then. I thought you meant Talon. My woman ain't making cookies for another man when she hasn't even made her old man any yet."

"Declan." I knew she'd rolled her eyes when she said my name like that, like I was being foolish.

"Hell no, woman. My cookies."

She sighed. "Okay, fine. Just Saxon. Then I'll tell Zara how Talon helped and she'll make him some cookies."

I scoffed, "That's fine with me." After kissing her neck, I added, "We're gonna have to watch the two of them."

"Who?" she asked as she shifted and snuggled deeper into me, placing her hand on my arm that lay around her waist.

"Saxon and Nary."

"What? Why?"

"She has a crush on him."

"I could tell when she spoke of him. But why should we keep an eye on them?"

"Seriously?"

"Ah, yes."

"She's a girl, your girl, which means in a way my girl, and he's a guy. I was that age once, I know all he wants to do is fuck. He ain't fuckin' Nary over or I'd have to kill him." Her body started to shake in my arms. "Malinda?" I asked and prayed she was laughing at me instead of what I thought she could be doing...crying.

"Are you cryin'?" I demanded. She didn't answer so I got up to my elbow and made her roll to her back. She had her hands over her face. I pried them away and saw tears running down her face. "Why are you crying?"

"Y-you."

"Me what? I made you cry? Fuck, do I need to beat myself up?"

She laughed then. "No, it's just... you care."

My head jutted back. She'd shocked the shit outta me. "Ah, yeah, I care or else I wouldn't have had my fingers deep inside you and I wouldn't be in this bed staying the night with my woman."

"But… you don't only care for me. You care about my kids too."

Rolling my eyes, I said, "Of fuckin' course I do. They came from you, which means they're a part of you. Plus, they're cool kids, not hard to care for them."

She smiled up at me, her eyes soft. She placed her hand on my cheek. "Thank you."

Smiling, I leaned into her. "Christ, woman, you don't need to thank me."

"But I want to."

"Okay, still you don't have to."

"However, I wanted to."

"Fuck me. Okay, woman, I get the feelin' if I keep goin', so will you, so I'll shut the fuck up and we can get some sleep."

Her smile widened to show me her white teeth. "Okay, babe," she said and rolled back over. I took her back close to my front again. "Still, I think I won then," she added.

"Jesus." I laughed loudly.

My woman was fucking cute.

CHAPTER THIRTEEN

MALINDA

*T*hree more days passed since Nary had come home beaten and scared. She had returned to school and I was worried, but she reassured me she would be fine. My girl was strong if anything.

Three days also passed since Declan Stoke blew my mind in the bathroom and pulled all the right cords to my body. I wanted his hands on me again. I wanted to feel the connection we'd had that night. But I hadn't and I was pissed.

"All by myself" played over and over in my head since Declan Stoke hadn't showed his face for three days.

I knew he was busy. Apparently, there had been some stuff-ups at the site his construction company was working on. Yes, I had learned two days earlier, he owned a construction company with his biker brother, Fox, also known as Killer, and apparently, those stuff-ups had caused my man to be gone for two days.

No phone call.

No message.

Nothing passed on through his other biker brothers.

Nothing.

So I was annoyed and horny as a nun seeing Jensen Ackles' penis for the first time.

The next time I saw Declan Stoke, I just hoped he would be prepared for the consequences, because I was more than ready to jump his bones.

It had been thirteen years since I'd last had sex, and I was pretty much gagging for it. Especially since Declan Stoke came to mind. "You're shitting me," Mrs Cliff gasped. I looked up from the kitchen bench where I had been cutting tomatoes for lunch sandwiches to see her shocked face from where she sat at the dining room table with Ivy. "Thirteen years since you've had your hole poked? Holy shit, I'm an old woman and it was only four day ago."

I grimaced. That was a picture I never wanted to imagine.

"I guess I said that aloud."

Ivy nodded. "I wondered why you were killing those tomatoes," she said and looked down at the chopping board, so of course I did also, then cringed at what I saw. Instead of slicing them, I had pretty much cut them into smithereens.

"I suppose I could turn them into tomato sauce for pasta?" I shrugged.

Ivy giggled. Mrs Cliff stood from the table, picked her

mobile and walked from the room.

"Where is she going?" I asked.

"Not sure," Ivy said just before we heard, "Where the hell are you? Do you know it's been thirteen years since my girl has gotten any? She'd been smiling big for a day, so you must have done something right. Then you disappear, leaving her horny and cranky. You better get your arse back here and fix this. Fix her by doing her."

Gasping, I yelled, "Mrs Cliff, no!" I raced from the room with Ivy behind me.

I was too late though. Standing in shock, I heard Mrs Cliff on the phone. She said a quick, "Right," and then hung up.

Gripping the back of the couch instead of Mrs Cliff's neck, I hissed, "Please tell me that wasn't Declan."

"It was Declan."

"Tell me then, that is wasn't *my* Declan."

"Well… he hasn't done you yet, so really is he your Declan? You know I could set you up with one of my boys if he ain't treating you right."

I glared at her and then sighed out, "Mrs Cliff."

"I think its sweet he's taking his time. Though, after what went on in the bathroom the other night, I highly doubted it would have taken him so long to be… um, intimate with you in a way when penetration would be involved if that silly mix-up at the site didn't happen. He's been working into the night to get things fixed. I just know he's working hard so he could take more time off to spend with you… not only to protect you, but to… oh, you know what I mean. Those men are always wanting their woman, and you my dear, have been claimed. He's had a taste of what you may be like in bed, now he wants more, I know he's just as eager as you are." Ivy smiled.

Throughout her long talk, I stared on with wide eyes and a gaping mouth.

"How... why... when?" I shook my head. "No, how do you know what went on in the bathroom?"

Her smile grew bigger and she said, "He told Fox and Fox told me. They talk about everything. Really, Stoke is the only one who Fox opens up to totally. I think it's sweet. They're like real brothers, not just biker brothers. He's the only one Fox has let see me naked... Oh, dear."

"Stoke has seen you naked?" I screeched.

"Um... it was the spur of the moment thing and way, way before you entered the picture, and it was only the once. Stoke happened to be in the room when Fox and I were getting hot and heavy. We forgot he was there, when we realised... we... um, kind of kept going." She blushed. "I'm sorry. I didn't know I liked to be watched until that moment."

Why did that send a tingle to my clit?

"Holy shit, that is damn hot." Mrs Cliff laughed.

Ivy must have forgotten she was there, she hid her hands in her face and said, "Fox is going to kill me."

"Ivy," I laughed and walked over to her. I placed my arm around her shoulders and said, "Don't worry about it. I won't say anything and neither will Mrs Cliff, or I won't let her in the house for a year."

"Bitch," Mrs Cliff hissed as she walked out the front door, slamming it behind her.

Ivy looked up at me and said, "You, um, you don't seem to mind that Stoke saw that?"

I shrugged. "It was before me so I don't mind at all. Besides, I would have been the same... I think." I smiled.

She giggled. "It does turn a person on more to be watched. Well, some people."

It was then we heard Harley pipes coming up the road. They stopped out the front when the front door opened, Mrs Cliff popped her head in and said, "You're welcome."

"For what?" I asked.

"This," she cackled and opened the door further as a frustrated-looking Stoke filled it. "Ivy dear, let's get the fuck out of here before they hump like rabbits in front of us."

"Declan?" I uttered.

"Seriously? Thirteen years?" he barked. He was standing with his clenched hands at his sides, his feet apart slightly and his chest taut, like he was holding himself back.

Oh. My.

Over his head, I spotted Mrs Cliff give me wave before pulling Ivy out the door, who was giving me her thumbs up.

I smiled and laughed.

"Malinda," Declan growled. "Eyes on me right now."

I did. "Um, yes. Thirteen years."

"You been in a foul mood 'cause I haven't had you?"

Rolling my eyes, I said, "No."

"Malinda," he snapped, then smiled. "Have you been cranky 'cause you haven't had your man's cock?"

I snorted, bit my bottom lip and snapped, "Maybe."

"Then let's change that right now," he said in a low deep voice. Next, I was up over his shoulder and he was stalking to our bedroom. Once we were through the door, he kicked it closed and stood me on my feet. "I've been hard since I knew you wanted my cock in you, since I found out off an old fuckin' lady that it's been thirteen years. As soon as she spoke, I started for my bike. When she hung up the phone, I was on my Harley and riding to my woman with a hard cock in my jeans. This... I can't be slow and gentle. You down with this or do you want to wait until I calm a bit? Which could take a fuckin' long time. Warning though, you may have to run from me."

I reached up, placed my hands on his cheeks, looked him in the eyes and said, "Declan Stoke, I want you to fuck me hard and fast. As long as you make me come."

"I reckon I could even bring two from you," he said with a wicked smile. We raced to get undressed. I won of course and quickly lay back on the bed. Declan nearly fell as he pulled his boots off because he was too busy eyeing me.

As soon as he was free of clothes, he ordered, "Spread 'em, love."

Even though I blushed, I did as he said and spread my legs apart. He licked his lips as he palmed his already massive, hard cock. I ran my eyes over his body, took in his scars on his lower stomach and chest. I'd seen them three days ago in the bathroom, but my mind didn't really take them in. Until he was standing before me, allowing me the time to take him all in. I knew they were there because he had protected not only his brother, but his brother's woman as well. That made me care for him so much more.

Declan Stoke was a good man.

And he was all my man.

He slowly climbed onto the bed, his hand leaving his dick, even though I whimpered my complaint; I liked watching him touch himself. He placed his hands on my legs and glided them up until he was massaging the inside of my upper thighs.

"I'm gonna eat you first, love. I've wanted a taste of your pussy since the first time I saw you." A thrill shivered through my body.

I closed my eyes and brought my hips up, his invitation. He chuckled and I felt his hot breath against the top of my mound. I shivered in anticipation.

On the first lick, from the bottom to the top of my opening, I gripped the sheets under me and moaned.

"You like my mouth on you?" he growled.

"Yes, Declan, God, yes," I replied.

"Good, I fuckin' love your taste," he said, then went for it. No more talking was involved, his mouth was busy devouring my pussy. One second his tongue was in my pussy hole, running all around it, in the next second, it was driving my clit wild, running over and around it. It didn't take him long to draw a climax from my body.

"Declan," I screamed through it. I slumped back ready to rest, though he didn't let me. His large body came up over me.

Yes, resting can wait. I was going to get some and that took priority over rest any day. It was more special because it was with Declan. A man I deeply cared for.

I watched through hooded eyes as he gripped himself and lined his cock up with my snatch. With one thrust, he was deep inside of me. I threw my head back, gripped his forearms and moaned. His cock was a tight fit, but it was perfect.

"Fuck," he grunted.

I wrapped my legs around his hips as he pumped fast into me and pulled back even faster. He had been right. This was going to be hard and swift, but it was going to be good. My lower stomach started to cry in joy as my pussy walls tightened more than I thought possible, because already, another climax was building.

I reached up and wrapped my arms around his neck. He collapsed on top of me, but his hips never relented; they kept going, in return, his big cock fucked me.

"Kiss me," I ordered.

He did, but not before I caught his satisfied smile. His mouth met mine, as we kissed and fucked, I ran my hands all over his body, his neck, back and arse. It was a damn fine.

Suddenly, he pulled back to lean on his hands and look down at me. "Fuckin' beautiful," he groaned as he watched his cock punish my pussy in the most delicious way. I wished I could see what he was focusing on, but watching him enjoying it was enough. "You're soaked, so fuckin' good. Tight, hell, you're tight."

"Just for you," I moaned as my pussy gripped Declan's erection and then pulsated around it as my climax crashed over me. My inner walls clamped down around his cock. I knew he felt it when his head went back and he cried out, thrusting faster into me.

"Fuck, yes," he grunted. His cock swelled inside of me and next I felt his seed filling me. He collapsed once again on top of me, only to roll to the side seconds later. When he slipped out from me, he said, "Shit, I forgot to use protection."

Panting, I patted him on the chest. "Don't worry about it. I'm covered and clean."

"Good, me too. I want at least a year of us before I get you pregnant."

My body froze.

He wanted kids?

With me?

Oh. My.

"Malinda?"

"Hmm?"

"By the way your claws are in my arm, you're either freaked the fuck out right now, or don't want any more kids and are too scared to tell me."

"We've only been together for—"

"I don't fuckin' care. My brothers knew and now I know."

"Knew what?"

"Knew when the right one came along."

My hand went to my chest as my heart started to mend.

For so many years it had been broken, I never thought it would be fixed. I never thought I would get it all again and better.

But I have and I never would have thought it would from another biker.

But it was, and I couldn't be happier.

Mattie had been right all along.

I just had to trust.

CHAPTER FOURTEEN

ONE MONTH LATER

MALINDA

*I*nsanity was slowly making its way into my mind. I was bored out of my brain and I was sick of holding up Talon and his men, who were on twenty-four-seven babysitting duty, watching over my children and me. I wanted Oscar found and...disposed of in any way possible. Lan had just visited yesterday and told me they still had no leads as to where the infuriating man was.

Nobody was coming up with anything.

Lan was a surprise. He was a nice, very 'steamy dream', looking man. Whenever Declan heard he was coming around, he made sure he was at the house, and when he was, it was like Lan enjoyed rubbing him the wrong way. He did it by flirting outrageously with me and when he did it, I unfortunately, became a stuttering, blushing fool.

The previous day had been worse, compared to the other two times over the past month.

I'd opened the door to see Lan in all his edible glory leaning against my porch railing opposite the door. He wore dark jeans, and a white shirt, which hugged his toned body. I was ashamed when a blush formed on my cheeks, after he chuckled and I may have sighed. Still, nothing he did or said sent my heart into a freaking frenzy like it had when Declan walked into a room, or called, or spoke, or when he touched me... hell, every time he did anything, even watching him brush his teeth turned me on.

Declan must have heard his cousin laugh, and knew I reacted in a way I shouldn't have. Therefore, I wasn't surprised to have him at my back in the next second, his arm around my waist where he picked me up and carried me to the couch in the living room. Once there, he sat down first with me on his lap.

Lan walked in slowly, closed the front door and walked into the living room where he sat across from me on my coffee table. His hand came out laid on my knee. Declan growled behind me. Amused, Lan smiled, I once again blushed; only that time, I followed through with a giggle.

"Fuckin' hell," Declan hissed behind me. "You're lucky, Malinda, that I know you take my cock every night and only think of who's inside you, not of fuckin' him."

I turned in his lap and glared. "That is crude, Declan," I snapped. "But true. He's just real pretty is all."

Lan groaned, and Declan burst out laughing. "Hell, woman, you just made my day. See, cousin, you're just *real pretty.*"

"Mally, baby," Lan said. "You could have gone with ruggedly handsome. Hell, anything is better than pretty."

Stepping into the kitchen, I shook the thoughts of the previous day away. Instead, I thought of how much I was sick of staying at home. I was sick of my house; I never thought that would be possible. I loved my home. But being inside it all the time was killing me. They didn't want me exposed in case anything happened.

The men were governed by their experiences involving their women. When the illustrious pussy posse went through their ordeals—Zara, Deanna and Ivy had all been taken when the men thought they had them covered—it had done things to them, making them more cautious. Clary was the only one who sent herself out there as bait, I could see why. She had been in the same situation as me, stuck in places for long amounts of time.

The thought of doing what Clary did crossed my mind. However, I wasn't brave enough to attempt at being bait, even though I knew I'd have all the Hawks' men at my back. The other reason was that I knew Declan wouldn't go for it.

At least one worry I had in the past month was somewhat resolved and I was so happy for it: Nary was better. What helped was that Malcolm *had* disappeared, so she didn't have to see his face again at school. What also helped was that wherever Nary went in school, Saxon was always following.

I'd had him around for his cookies. He was a quiet boy, a

year ahead of my daughter and graduating soon. He'd just turned eighteen last week, not that I knew at the time, if I had, I would have done something for it. That was probably why no one warned me.

Declan was right. The crush Nary had on Saxon was obvious, and I had an inkling that Saxon felt the same way; however, he never showed it. Even at school, when he followed her, he was quiet and standoffish. Still, I saw the way he looked at Nary when he thought no one was watching him. There was definitely something there. I could only hope he was smart enough to wait until she was eighteen or back off altogether. I had a feeling that Saxon Black could break my daughter's heart more than any other boy.

I went into the living room after grabbing a coffee and sat down to turn on my show. Yes, I resorted to watching soap operas during the day. Why? Because I was going batshit crazy with boredom.

The house phone rang. I leaned to the end of the couch to pick it up from its cradle on the small table that also held a lamp. "Hello?"

"Love," came Declan's deep voice and my heart took off with a deeper thump, thump.

"Hey." I smiled.

"What are you doing?"

"Um, I'm about to watch Fredric tell Joyce that he has always loved her, even though she was married to his father for a year before he died."

"Fuck," Declan hissed.

"What?"

"Expect a call soon," he said, then hung up. I took the phone away from my ear and looked at it. That was weird.

Next, I heard a key in the lock at the front door, when it opened there stood Warden. He took a step in, holding a phone to his ear. He looked at me, then the TV, then back to me and said, "It's bad. She's watching some shit on TV, drinking coffee and wearing some ratty old tee, Ugg boots and tracksuit pants."

What the?

"Yep, call them in. Something needs to be done," he said, then hung up.

"Warden—" I started, but didn't finish when he held his hand up in front of him to silence me.

"Don't wanna hear it, Mally. You need a fuckin' hobby while under house arrest. This can't go on. You know I love you like a sister, but you look like shit and you're watching it as well." He stood there with accusing eyes and his hands on his hips.

Okay, so in the past week, I may have gone extra crazy. My routine consisted of getting up, making lunch for the children, saying a goodbye to Declan, tidying the house, maybe have a shower and then veg out in from of the TV. I didn't care what I wore, whether I smelled or ate. Until it came to four when I knew the children were coming home. I didn't want to seem too out of it in front of them, so I tidied myself up a little.

Maybe Declan knew more than I thought he did. Rolling my eyes at myself, I should have guessed his biker brothers would rat me out eventually.

Warden cleared his throat and snapped before he disappeared out the front door again. "Expect a call soon."

Again... what the?

In that moment, the home phone rang, causing me to jump and drop the damn thing onto the floor. Once I picked it up, I answered with a suspicious, "Hello?"

"Hey, girl," Ivy said.

"What's going on Ivy?" I asked.

"Well, this is how it is." I sat back on the couch getting comfortable for Ivy's long talk, "Stoke rang Killer, and in return, he rang me. But this was after Stoke talked to Warden, Billy and Dive. They've all been worried about you this week. Stoke thinks you need some time out with the girls. He's right, but it's not like we haven't been telling him that for weeks now. I mean, it's only so long he can keep you to himself. I know he's being greedy and wanting your attention for just himself at night. Anyway, I'm getting off track. He enlisted the posse to come grab you tonight for a girls' night. Yay! Anyway, Mrs Cliff is coming to your house to look after the kids. There will be brothers there, like always, standing guard. While you, me and the girls...we're all heading to one of Talon's strip joints to get our drink on. It's going to be so much fun." She stopped to take a breath and someone said something in the background. "Oh, yes, Clary also said that drunk sex is the best sex. Though, those biker boys are dang awesome just regularly, don't you think?"

"Um, yes."

"That's what I'm talking about, sister. So, be ready at seven, girl. Your man will be there to pick you up."

"Okay?"

"Yay," she cried into the phone and hung up.

Girls' night.

I was going to have a girls' night. I'd never had one before. It had always been just Tank, his friends and me.

Jumping up from the couch, I squealed, did a jig and ran to my room to get ready—even though it was only two in the afternoon.

WHEN THE CHILDREN ARRIVED HOME, I was in my bedroom still going through my clothes. I just didn't know what to wear. They'd come into the room, and at the same time their eyes bugged out. So, I may have had a lot of clothes thrown around. After shaving and showering, I sat in my robe looking forlorn.

Josh slowly backed out of the room and bolted. Something any guy would do. Nary started giggling and soon I joined in.

"I just don't have a clue," I said through laughter.

"How long has it been since you went out?" I'd already texted her when she was at school and told her the night's plans.

Slumping back on the bed with a sigh, I admitted, "Nearly eighteen years."

"Wow, Mum."

"I know. How do I do this? Should I even go?"

"Heck yes, you need this. At least we get out of the house for school. You're stuck here all the time."

"I—"

"Where is she?" We heard Mrs Cliff ask and then Josh mumbled something.

I sat up just before she filled the doorway. She took one look and whistled. "Holy shit, did a bomb go off in here?"

"Mrs Cliff you're early."

"Your young boy rang me and said you needed help. You look stressed out and I can see why. What you trying to do? Pick hooker clothes for tonight? I can help with that."

As I took in her red sweater and brown track pants, I wasn't sure Mrs Cliff could help. She didn't exactly have good choice in clothes.

"Don't looked freaked out. I have damn good taste. I only dress like this 'cause my man likes it."

She had a man?

"You have a man?" Nary asked as shocked as I was.

"Several actually. The men can't get enough of me. Now, tonight, you wear that, that and that." She pointed to my skinny jeans, a pink silk shirt and ankle boots. "You're going to a slutty place, but that doesn't mean you need to look slutty like those others. My Malinda has class as well. Right, we're done here. Girl, you come with me while your mumma gets pretty; could take a while, we'll order some takeout." She started back down the hall. Nary grinned at me and followed Mrs Cliff.

CHAPTER FIFTEEN

MALINDA

*W*hen Stoke picked me up right at seven, I took one look at him and asked if we could stay home and if the children could go to Mrs Cliff's instead. He looked damn fine, as in *Fine* with a capital F. He had on dark jeans, boots and a white shirt... I had never seen my man in a white shirt. I licked my lips and asked once again if we could stay home. He laughed, eye fucked me in my get-up, and said no. After a quick goodnight to all, we made our way to his pick-up, waving at Dodge and a mad-looking Griz.

Once seated, I turned to my man and asked, "What's wrong with Griz?"

"He's not happy Hell Mouth is going out tonight, or that Mrs Cliff is in the house."

I couldn't help but giggle. Deanna had told me when they went over for dinner a while ago, Mrs Cliff had tested Griz out for her adopted granddaughter, asking him if he wanted to sleep with her. When Griz declined, she then asked if he found Pink, the singer, spunky enough to fuck— yes, they were her words. Griz nearly choked on his beer and coughed out, "No! What the fuck, woman? I'm married and I'm very goddamn happy." She was proud of his response so she gave her blessing for their relationship to continue.

Talon's strip club was all the way out near Geelong. When we pulled onto the highway, four other cars behind us joined, as well as at least ten Harleys. I looked to Declan and all he said was, "Precaution."

On the way there, Declan and I played twenty questions regarding mundane things.

"Favourite colour?" I asked on my fourth go.

"Green. Favourite sex position?"

"Declan," I snapped.

"Come on, love. There's no rules to what I can ask."

"Fine," I grumbled and looked out my window, hiding my smile. "I, um, I like to be on top."

Declan's deep chuckle filled the car. "You like to take charge. Sounds good to me, but don't be disappointed if I take over in the end."

Flicking out my tongue, I licked my lower lip wet. "I won't mind." Then I giggled, shaking my head and I asked, "What about you?"

"Is that your next question?"

"Yes."

"Okay," he grinned. "With you, love, I like it anyway. Standing, lying, you on top or me; fuck, even sideways. Eating you out even works for me. I swear I could come from the sweet sounds that fall from your sexy lips."

Wow.

"Is it getting hot in here?" I asked, because I was certainly cooking.

Declan let out a burst of laughter. "Don't worry, babe. You'll be smokin' later after I'm finished with you."

"Um...awesome." I smiled. He laughed again.

"We're nearly there. You got any more questions for me?"

I had a million. Over the last month, we'd talked and had deep and meaningful conversations, but I still found there was a lot to discover about Declan Stoke.

"Are... ah, are you happy?"

He took his eyes off the road to meet mine, I saw his were soft. He turned his attention back to the road before answering with, "Yeah, love. Before I met you, I was like, 'fuck women'. I couldn't be bothered with them. I'd been shit on in the past, but once I got to know you, fuck, even before that. When I saw you the first time you came to the compound...I just felt you were different, you're classy, sweet and sexy. You're so much more than the whores I used to take. You're special and I wanted you for me. When you finally caved, I was so fuckin' thankful."

My whole body melted.

He took my hand from my leg, picked it up and kissed it. He sat our joined hands on his leg. "What about you, love? You happy?"

Was I happy?

Even though I was stuck in the house, even though I had a black dooming cloud over my head, and no doubt more trouble coming my way, I knew the answer.

"Yes," I uttered. "I know nothing is normal right now, but... I'm happy. You've made me happier than I've ever been."

"Fuck, love," he growled. "If we didn't have people following us, I'd pull over and fuck you so hard right now. We're making this night an early one. I want to go home and cherish each and every inch of you."

"That sounds amazing," I said.

The best part was Declan Stoke calling it home. He classed the house my children and I lived in as home. That made me smile.

"Declan?"

"Yeah, Malinda?" he asked and gave my hand a squeeze.

"Where...um, before you came to live with us, where did you live?"

"So I am living with you?"

"Yes," I said straight away.

"Glad you said that, love. You worried?"

"That it's only new and been a little more than a month and that you could possible break my heart? Hell yes."

He chuckled. "So am I, but reverse that, Malinda. Still, what I know is that I don't like being away from you. I want to continue waking up with you, seeing your kids grow and help out with shit. I like where this is going. We're gonna have crap times, love, but I reckon we can get through them. We just gotta stick at it. You with me on that?"

"Definitely, Declan."

"Good. Now to answer your question, I have a house. We'll leave it for another six months, see how strong we're going, and then I'll look at selling it. You down with that?"

"Sounds like a plan."

"Brilliant." He smiled and pulled into a large gravel carpark. Just in front of that was a huge two-story brick building, one that looked like an old factory, but revamped into something else, something better. It was full of life already, lights blaring, music pumping. I could tell Talon's business was profiting from the already busy carpark and it was only eight.

"Right, this is how it's gonna go down." He pulled to a stop as the other vehicles parked around us. "You don't leave me and my brothers' sight. You stick with the women like glue. You don't go anywhere on your own, no matter what. Even if someone comes up to you and says some shit, you don't listen if you don't know and trust them. You get me? You're with Hawks or their women, or we leave."

"Got it, babe." I nodded with a smile.

"Don't make me regret this night, Malinda."

"I won't. Promise."

He studied me and then grinned. "Yeah, you're my good girl. Let's do this before your women start breakin' shit on my car."

"Com'on, dude, you get her all the time. Give her to us now," Deanna yelled from outside.

"Shit. If they suggest any dangerous shit, do not listen." I giggled and kissed him quickly. He pulled back and ordered, "I mean it."

Rolling my eyes, I said, "I know." My door opened and I was pulled from the car by an over excited Julian.

"OMG, girl, I am so ready to get my groove on. I wonder if the strippers will let me on stage. I don't mind taking my clothes off at all."

"Shit," Declan drew out, which caused me to giggle.

I swear there were at least twenty Hawks' men surrounding us. Once an over-excited Julian yanked me out of the car by, I was quickly shuffled from his arms into Talon's, who walked me right in and up some stairs to the VIP area. There he sat me down in a huge-arse booth that could seat at least twenty people. The table was bigger than my kitchen, when I looked left, I found out why. There were four other booths like the one I sat at, and the other four had girls dancing on top of them. Soon, Deanna, Ivy, Julian, Mattie, Clary, Zara and an older woman I didn't know, sat around the table with me.

"This place kicks arse," Deanna said.

"I have to agree. I've never been to a strip club before. I didn't think it would be this... tasteful. Oh, goodness, yoo-hoo!" the older woman called to a waitress, who in her topless attire, waltzed over with a smile upon her face. "I just wanted to say that I think you have a wonderful body."

"Thank you, darling."

The older woman across from me then held out her hand to the waitress and said, "I'm Nancy, Talon's mother-in-law."

Oh. My.

"Well, it's great to meet you. My name's Teresa." The platinum, double Fs, blue-eyed woman said as she shook her hand.

"Can I ask, are they real?" Nancy gestured the double Fs.

"They sure are. You wanna feel them?" Teresa placed her free hand on the table and leaned in.

"Kitten," I heard growled.

But my eyes were all for Nancy as she raised her hand and probably would have went for a good squeeze if Zara hadn't quickly reach out and grabbed her wrist saying, "Mum, maybe groping one of Talon's employees isn't a good thing. I'm sure there's a no touch policy or something."

Nancy leaned back and rolled her eyes. "Talon, you would let your mother-in-law have a feel, right?"

"Fuck me," was hissed. I looked up at the end of the booth to see Talon standing there with a scowl upon his face. Though the men around him seemed very amused, those men included my man, Blue and Killer. "Nancy, no."

"Tell me again how Mum got invited?" Mattie asked.

"She didn't," Ivy whispered over me to Mattie, who was sitting on my other side. "She invited herself. Your dad tried to stop her, but she wouldn't hear of it. She wanted him to come along so she could reap the benefit from it, he said he was too old for... excuse my language, shit like this. He thinks he'd look like a dirty old pervert if he came and watched women his daughter's age dancing around half-naked."

I definitely wanted to meet Mattie's dad. I had a feeling Nancy was going to be a hoot, but I wanted to see her and her husband's dynamics. That would be more entertainment than those TV soaps.

"Sweetheart," Julian started, I felt Mattie stiffen beside me, then groan. "We'll meet you in your break-room later. Then no one will be witness. Can't have Nancy miss the experience of her first groping. He eyed Teresa's breasts. "They look heavy, baby-girl."

Teresa giggled and said, "They are, sugar. I'll show you later how heavy."

"Kitten," Talon growled again. "Reel your posse in, woman."

"Got it, honey. Guys, there will be no touching tonight and that's final. We're in my hubby's place of business. We have to act responsibly," she ordered, then a smile lit her face and she waved, yelling, "Hey, Livi, over here, babe."

A tall, green-eyed woman with red hair, styled in a pixie cut, turned toward Zara when she called. The redhead beamed a wide, big smile and came strutting over. Her hips sway seductively in her short-short black leather skirt. To top it off, she wore black stilettos and a dark green halter-top.

When she reached the table, Talon let out a low, "Livi, don't."

I looked to Zara to see she was smiling. Then I glanced back to see Livi ignore Talon's warning tone, lean over the table and peck Zara on the lips. She pulled back, grinned wickedly and said, "Honey-pie, how is my girl doing?"

"Boss, you been holding out on some information?" Blue queried.

Instead of answering, Talon gripped the back of Livi's

skirt and pulled her back, away from his wife. "Stop pulling your shit and get back to work," he ordered Livi with a scary voice.

But Livi just snorted and looked to Zara. "Is he like this at home?"

Zara scoffed. "I only allow it in the bedroom."

"Jesus motherfucking Christ. Are you all Goddamn deaf? Livi, get lost. Teresa, get drink orders. Me and my brothers will be at the bar keepin' an eye on things. Stay out of trouble...fuck, look who I'm talking to. Try to stay out of trouble. Nancy, Julian, if you want to come here again, you will not touch any of the women tonight, even if they are on a fuckin' break. Let's go," he said. Talon and his men turned and made their way to the bar. Stoke quickly sent me a wink and smile, before he followed his president.

It was then I could tell why Talon was the president. Yes, Declan Stoke was scary when he was angry. But Talon Marcus, he was nightmare material. I looked to Zara with wide eyes. She grinned at me and shook her head. "Don't worry about him. He's tame at home."

Yeah... sure.

LATER IN THE NIGHT, I had just collapsed into the booth with Clary and Ivy, after dancing my feet off like Lady Gaga on crack, when two older men we didn't know walked up. I glanced to the bar to see Stoke and Blue coming our way. I looked to the dance floor to see Zara, Nancy and Deanna still grooving it out with some strippers. Mattie was downstairs with Julian, keeping an eye on him while he danced with the strippers on stage. Apparently, while he was in the toilets earlier, they all saw his sweet dance moves and asked him to teach them a few things. Of course, Julian was more than willing.

"Ladies, which one of you is Malinda?" Mr Tall, Broad and Rugged asked. He looked around forty, like his friend next to him. They also had in common, buzz haircuts, tattoos that cover their arms, and they were both dressed in jeans, tees and army boots. The main difference was one had hard dark brown eyes and the other had light blue eyes.

"Who wants to know?" Clary asked with a glare. She stood from the table. They backed up a step to make room for her, just as Declan and Blue arrived. My man sat stiffly next to me while Blue slid his arm around Clary's waist and brought her back against his chest.

"Who the fuck are you?" Blue asked.

"We're here for back-up to watch Malinda May."

"If you're here to do that, then shouldn't you know what she looks like?" Clary asked.

The blue-eyed man turned his cold stare to Clary. "Sergeant only had a photo of her when she was turned away from the camera and another from tonight as she left, but it was dark."

"I'm Malinda," I said. The men were all getting too tense. I didn't want the situation to blow up over something so little. "Can I ask who Sergeant is?"

The other man spoke up in a deep voice. "Beth Cliff."

I gasped. "Mrs Cliff is your sergeant?"

They both smirked. The blue-eyed one added, "Was, that

was a while ago now. We've just gotten off duty or we would've been here as soon as she called." He looked from Blue to Stoke and then held out his hand to my man. "Sergeant said you were in charge of Malinda, Declan Stoke, right?" Declan gave him a chin lift with the handshake. "I'm Trevor Boon and this here is Dallas Gan."

"Good to meet you both, but as you can see, my brothers and I have everything under control," Declan said after he shook both of their hands and leaned back against the booth. His arm slid around my shoulders again, where he brought me snugly against him.

"That may be so, but when Beth asks anything, we deliver, no matter what."

"Why?" Ivy asked. "I mean Mrs Cliff is a great lady, and she must have been one heck of a sergeant, but I don't get why years later you're both still willing to do anything for her."

The men looked at each other, and when Dallas nodded, Trevor turned back to us and said, "She saved our arse a long time ago, hell, a few times actually. If it wasn't for her, we wouldn't be alive today."

Ivy's hand went to her heart. "That is so sweet," she breathed. "It must have been fun working with her."

The men smirked and Dallas said, "You could say that. She's a tough person to get along with, but once you were in her fold, she was loyal."

Deanna suddenly showed and sat in the booth breathing heavily. "God damn, I haven't shaken my arse like that for a long time. Tell me who I have to screw to get a drink around here." Blue glared down at her. "Oh, fuck off, dude, not like I'd actually screw anyone, my man is enough for me." She stopped, looked at the men standing beside Clary and Blue, who were smiling down at her, and then she snapped, "Who the fuck are these two thugs and do I have to beat the shit outta them?"

"Are you related to Beth?" Trevor asked.

We all burst out laughing. It really was uncanny how Mrs Cliff and Deanna were so similar.

"Who's Beth?" Deanna glared.

"Mrs Cliff," Clary said through her laughter.

"Oh." I watched Deanna smile. "Nope, but she wants to adopt me." Her smile widened.

"I can see why," Dallas deadpanned.

Something in Declan's pocket vibrated. He moved to the side to pull out his phone. When he put it to his ear, he said, "Speak."

Mrs Cliff was loud enough that I even heard her. "You send my boys away I will make your life hell. It's not that I don't fuckin' trust you and the biker hotties. I just trust my boys more. I know what they are capable of. Until I see one of you kill a man with his bare hands, like I have with those two, I want them on the job. You tell them what to do, where to be and they'll do it. You get me, boy? Or else think of me as your new neighbour from Hell."

"You're not already?"

"Get fucked," she snapped, but I knew she was smiling. She liked Stoke and I knew, deep, deep, deep down, he liked her.

"Fine."

"Good," she said and then hung up.

"Beth?" Trevor asked with a lip twitch. Dallas was nice enough to hide his laugh with a pretend cough.

"You're both downstairs. Keep your eyes and ears open. The gay guy on the stage and the one with him are Hawks." They eyed my man to see if he was serious. Declan answered their look with, "Don't fuckin' ask. The women are crazy for them. Go meet the other brothers around, then head down there," Declan ordered.

"Done," both Trevor and Dallas said. They turned to leave, which was when we heard Dallas say, "We should have fuckin' got here sooner. Then I would have had a chance with Malinda."

I blushed. Declan turned to me, saw my blush and said, 'Fuck me, I can't take you anywhere without attracting men."

CHAPTER SIXTEEN

MALINDA

*A*fter a few more hours of fun, dancing and copious amounts of alcohol, I was sitting in the booth laughing with Ivy about something, though I couldn't really recall what it was. But it had been funny. *I think.* I was on a high, and surprised to see even though we were in a strip club with nearly naked women dancing or walking around, the Hawks men still only had eyes for their women. Well, the ones who had partners did, the others not so much. Still, they all focused on what they were told to do, so they kept their minds in the game and protected us Hawk women.

Guilt tinged my thoughts earlier, until Ivy must have read my mind and ordered me not to worry. She told me the men lived for this stuff. They ate, pooped and breathed the bad-arse biker life. They didn't care they had to watch out for me. Even a few, who'd heard the conversation, agreed and told me not to be stupid.

It was then I shrugged it off and had another drink.

Talon had already left, taking Zara, Nancy and Deanna with him. All that was left was Julian, Mattie and Clary, who were at that point, downstairs in the change rooms, doing makeovers with the strippers who weren't dancing. I joined them earlier, until Ivy dragged me out for another dance. After three songs, we'd exhausted ourselves and were now laughing our butts off while sitting in the booth.

Ivy nudged me in the ribs with her elbow. I looked to her and she gestured with her chin toward the bar. Glancing over, I spotted what she was talking about. Killer and Declan were deep in conversation. They were close, their foreheads nearly touching. Declan looked...wary about what Killer was saying. I could tell from where I sat that he was tense. It made me wonder what they were discussing.

"Looks intense," I said.

"Yeah, makes you wonder what it's about." She paused and then added, "Maybe it's just about work?"

"Could be, but I doubt it."

It was then they both looked over at us. Ivy waved around me, causing Killer to smirk and shake his head. My eyes moved to my man; his heated gaze made me catch my breath. He sent me a chin lift. I smiled and winked back. His lips moved. I knew he was talking to Killer when I witnessed Killer smile and nod.

They started for the table. My heart raced higher and higher with every step my man took. My libido and wet panties told me it was time to go. I needed to have my wicked way with Declan Stoke.

"Cupcake," Killer said. I always loved how he called her that. He held out his hand and Ivy squeezed by. Killer looked to me and then to Stoke before he said, "See ya soon."

Declan replied with, "Yep," then he sat down next to me while Killer led Ivy away.

"Are they going? I didn't get a chance to say goodbye to Ivy."

"They aren't going, love."

"Oh, so um...where are they going?"

Declan didn't answer me; instead, he turned to me and asked, "You havin' a good night, babe?"

Grinning, I said, "Yes."

"I'm glad."

"Do you want to go and dance?"

"Love." That one word sounded like I had just said the funniest thing.

"What?"

"Bikers don't dance."

I harrumphed and leaned into him more. "Talon danced with Zara."

He smirked, looked down at me and kissed my nose before he said, "You weren't watching it properly."

"What do you mean?"

He ran the back of his hand over my cheek, then threaded it into my hair where he pulled me closer and our lips dance together. The kiss caused me to rub my legs together to tame the thrill my pussy was feeling just from having his mouth on mine.

Once Stoke pulled back and smiled smugly, he said, "That was foreplay for Talon, not dancing."

I giggled. "Well, we could do that."

"Nah, we're gonna do something a little different."

My brows drew together. "What?"

He said nothing. He turned from me and searched the floor. I looked around also trying to find what he was looking for, when I saw Livi give Declan the thumbs up and a wide smile, he gave her a chin lift back and stood from the table. He held his hand out to me. I took it without question, because if we were leaving, I was all for it.

However, we didn't leave. Declan walked me to the far end of the bar where a door stood. He went to it, opened it and started down a dark hall to the end. There he opened another door that read 'Office', strutted through, dragging me with him, then he closed it.

"What are we doing, Deck?" I asked.

"Do you like porn?" he asked.

My eye widened. Had we come in here to watch porn? Not that I'd minded. I did like it; it always got me soaked in seconds. Still, I wasn't really comfortable watching it in Livi's office.

"Um," I started, licked my lips. With my hand still in his, he walked us over to the large, dark window to the left of the room. To the right lay a desk, chair, computer, bookcases and filing cabinets. "I don't mind it," I said and then added, "But I'd prefer to watch it at home."

"That's too bad," he said in a lust-filled voice. He positioned me to face the black window, which I found strange.

"Declan... I'd love to say the view's nice, but there's nothing to see."

It was then he reached to the right of the black window and flicked a switch. I gasped, but not from realising it was a one-way mirror which didn't work until Stoke turned it on. No, I gasped from the sight that was now in front of me.

There was just one table and chair in the middle of the room. The rest was barren, surrounded by white walls. Except for what was on that steel table.

Ivy was laying on top of it. She still had on her rocking white dress, bunched up to her hips with Killer between her spread legs going down on her. I didn't know if I should look away or what. I wanted to look away. I wanted to run from the room and not invade their very private situation. But I couldn't. My feet wouldn't move. I stood there trans-fixed to the one spot with my eyes gaping, my mouth ajar and my breath rapid.

Ivy arched and I watched her mouth part as a moan left her. I couldn't hear it, but I could see it. Killer gripped her thighs tighter. I was sure he'd leave a mark. He was naked from the waist up. Tattoos covered over his arms, however, I was sure he had more on his chest. The muscles in his back and arms were working double time. He liked what he was doing to his woman. No, he loved it. I watched as his head moved up and down, side to side just on the other side of Ivy's leg.

Ivy reached down and took hold of Killer's hair in a tight grasp. It was then I felt Declan's hand run down my back, causing me to shiver.

"It was Killer's idea." He spoke low, stepped closer to run

his tongue down my neck. "Ivy likes to be watched. So he wanted to do this for her." I nodded mutely. "I wasn't sure if you'd be into watching them... but fuck, love. I can see you're turned on. You cheeks are flushed. Your nipples are hard. Your chest is rising and falling so fast. I wonder... are you wet, love?"

I forced my gaze away from Ivy and Killer to look at Stoke. I was surprised to find his gaze already on me. He'd been looking at me, not them. Had he even watched any of it?

"I-I, um...." My brain wasn't firing on all cylinders.

Declan chuckled. "How about I find out for myself?" he asked. I gave him a small nod. "I want you to watch them, Malinda. Don't take your eyes off them, okay?"

Turning back to the window, I uttered, "Okay... but, does she know?"

"That you're watching?" I nodded. "Yeah, love, Fox would have told his woman. He keeps nothing from her. Do you care that she knows? Look at her, Malinda. She gets off on being watched."

He was right; she did. Ivy ran her hands up her stomach to her chest, where she squeezed her breasts. Killer must have said something because Ivy then smiled with her eyes closed and nodded.

As Declan stepped behind me, he unfastened my jeans as I watched Killer stand. The desire he felt for his woman was coming off him in waves; I swear I could see it. He loved his woman with every part of himself.

As Declan slowly slid his hand down the front of my

opened jeans, he felt just how wet I was. Killer then undid his own pants.

"You're fuckin' soaked, love," Declan groaned behind me. His other hand snaked up and gripped my breast. "Hand on the mirror, Malinda."

Panting, I did as I was told and was rewarded with a kiss to the neck. When Killer shoved his jeans to his knees, his large dick sprang free, I moaned because Stoke roughly shoved two fingers inside of me and thrust his jean-covered cock against my arse.

"He's going to fuck her hard, love."

"Hmm," I said. Christ, so much was going on; I was in overdrive. Declan tickled my clit. His hand moved from my breast and went to my jeans pulling them down my legs. I spread my legs wider and as Deck went back to finger fucking me, I watched through hooded eyes as Killer stepped between Ivy's legs, his hand wrapped around his cock as he lined himself up with Ivy's entrance.

"Declan," I whispered.

"What do you want?" he growled.

"You."

"How? Tell me, Malinda. How do you want me?"

Taking one hand from the mirror, I reached around and tugged at his jeans. He took my hand and placed it back onto the mirror. "Tell me," he growled deeply.

Killer leaned down and kissed his wife passionately. When he pulled away, he smiled down at her and then thrust forward, causing Ivy to cry out.

"Deck, please."

"All you have to do is tell me," he said, running his fingers from my dripping hole up to tease my clit.

I whimpered. I was so close to coming, but I wanted to do it with my man inside of me. "I want you to fuck me hard like Killer is Ivy," I uttered.

"Anything for you," he said, and I knew he was smiling. While I watched Killer lift Ivy's legs into the air, I felt Declan's hand at my arse as he quickly undid his jeans and pulled himself free. "Step back a couple, Malinda." I did and lifted my arse up further. He slapped it and I moaned loudly. At that point, I wouldn't even care if anyone heard. I needed to come and I needed my man's cock.

"So fuckin' beautiful," he groaned as he ran the tip of his dick through my wetness.

"Plea—" I started to beg until Stoke forced all of his cock into me. I cried his name. Filling me completely, my head fell back and I swore.

It felt right.

Wonderful.

Perfect.

"Yes," I cried. Declan gripped my hips and fucked me hard from behind.

"Watch them, love," he growled. I was sure he got off on me watching them, more than if he was to watch them. His right hand left my hip and threaded into my hair where he tugged and pulled my head up. "Watch them," he hissed.

I hadn't realised I wasn't watching. I was too involved in what I was feeling, how my pussy was taking my man's cock. He glided in and out in a frantic rhythm.

Opening my eyes, they changed positions. Killer had Ivy bent over the table, taking her from behind. Much like Declan was doing to me. Ivy's head was turned toward the mirror lying on the table. Her eyes half-mast and gazing our way. I was sure she could see us and I thought I wouldn't like it.

But I did.

"Fuck, yes," Declan hissed as even more wetness gushed from my pussy. My hands fell from the mirror as he put an arm across my chest and pulled my back against his chest. His hips pounding forward so his cock fucked me harder. His lips and mouth went to my neck, his breath heavy and hot. With his other hand, he slid to touch my clit, that was all it took.

My pussy clenched around my man's cock and I yelled out my release. While coming, I watched Ivy's eyes close and I knew she was coming just as hard as I was. Killer's head fell back, his face in a snarl as he pumped his seed into his woman.

Declan Stoke wasn't far behind. As my inner walls throbbed, his cock swelled from within and pulsed out his cum into my waiting pussy. A groan fell from his mouth and then, "Fuck, fuck, fuck, love."

STOKE

Never had I thought my woman would be into something like that. But as I lay in bed beside her after a night of booze and fun, I still found myself surprised with how

174

fucking lucky I was to have found and tagged Malinda May.

"Declan," she said with a tired voice.

"Yes, love?" I asked, tracing my fingers up and down her back as she lay naked on her stomach.

"You've never mention your family."

Smirking, I said, "No, and you've never mentioned yours."

She snorted. "Fine, I'll tell you mine if you tell me yours."

"Shoot," I said with a kiss to her shoulder.

"When my parents found out I was pregnant at the age of eighteen, they demanded I get an abortion. When I told them I wasn't, instead, I was moving in with Tank, they disowned me."

My hand stilled. Stupid fuckers missing out on such a good woman's life. "You mean to tell me they've never meet their grandkids?"

"Yes," she whispered to the room. I wound my arm around her waist. She kissed my shoulder because she knew I was pissed for her. "But it's too late now, anyway."

"Why?" I demanded. I wanted to hunt them down and tell them they were being demented for missing out on a good family.

"They died when I was twenty-two."

Well, at least I didn't have to hunt them.

"How?"

"They were flying their helicopter and crashed."

"Shit,"

"I know."

"You got any siblings?"

175

"Two brothers. I don't see them. They were two years younger than me. They're both living the life on our parents' money. Not that I care, because I don't. I would never want anything from anyone in my family. I have Nary and Josh. That's all I need."

"And me," I growled.

She giggled. "And you."

"So, I don't need to go and deal with your dumb-arse brothers?"

She laughed. "No, but thanks for the offer."

"My Malinda came from money and class?"

She groaned. "Yes, she did."

"I always knew you were classy, love. In your own special way, in a way that makes me hard every time I walk into a room. Though, you're not only classy, you're sweet, sexy, loyal, caring… fuck, there's a heap more, but just talking about it makes me want to fuck you."

"A-after you tell me about yours," she panted.

Chuckling I said, "Fine, but let's make it quick." I thrust my erection against her hip. She let out a small mew. She wanted me. Hell, that was the best motherfucking feeling. Shaking my head, I started, "My mother died when I was ten, leaving me with a drunk fuck for a father. He beat me, but then Lacy, Lan's mum, cottoned on when I was fifteen. She called the cops on my dipshit dad. He went to jail. I lived with Lacy and Lan for three years. I moved out and patched in to Hawks. Seven years later, Killer and I started out own construction company. The rest is history. The end. Now open those sweet legs, woman. Your old man needs some lovin'."

Quickly moving, I was on top of her back in a second nestling my cock into her arse crack and flung the sheet to the floor. She spread her legs more in a laugh but then said, "Stop."

Dammit, I did. I knew she'd have questions. I laid down, covered her back with my weight.

"Make it quick, Malinda. I'm about to explode."

Giggling, she said, "I can't have that now."

"No, so hurry," I growled. Fuck it, she could question me all she wanted, but I had to be inside her for it. Up on my hands, I stared down at the beauty that lay under me. Her arse was magnificent. Instead of admiring it more, I took hold of my cock and slid it home, straight into her wet, tight pussy.

She moaned. "Deck... I, oh, God."

Grinning, I pulled back out slowly and pushed in with force, watching her hands clench into the sheet under her. "Ask your questions, love."

"I-I, um, it's hard."

"Thank you." I chuckled, slowing my assault on her pussy; instead, just dipping my dick in and out so fuckin' slowly, I was gonna go crazy from it.

"N-not, yes. God, not what I meant," she mumbled into the sheets.

"Malinda, you better Goddamn hurry with those questions."

"O-okay, oh, honey, that feels so good," she panted. "Um, ah questions. Why, ah...leave Lan's house?"

Jesus Christ, I wanted her questions, but I didn't think it'd be hard to answer, I swear my brain was currently in my cock because all it was saying was 'Fuck her, fuck her hard, slow. Enjoy, aw… shit, I'm gonna cum.'

"Fuck, love, you feel so good," I grunted. "I'll answer this one question, then were done," I growled, leaned on my elbows and paused my movements. She whimpered her complaint, but there was no way I could think straight as her pussy sucked off my cock. "It was great there, but I was going through some shit. I didn't think I was good enough to stay there and be treated with kindness and such. So I left. Still, I visit her about once a month." Taking a breath, I added, "Before you ask, I haven't seen my father since he got out of jail. He lives in Sydney now somewhere. I really don't give a fuck where." Biting her shoulder, she moaned and I asked, "We done now?"

"I hope you just mean talking? Because yes, we're done, but you still have to finish."

"Yeah, love, and how do you want me to finish?"

"Fuck me hard, but I want you to come in my mouth." I had to chuckle because she looked so shocked that came out of her mouth.

Hell, I was glad it did, the thought of coming in her mouth dried up my balls and I had to pull out. She yelled my name in anger. Until I flipped her over and placed my dick at her lips. Smiling, she took me inside and sucked just in time for my cum to squirt out.

"Christ, woman, I'll make it up to you."

After she sucked me dry, she said, "You'd better."

I did. Two fuckin' times.

CHAPTER SEVENTEEN

THREE WEEKS LATER

STOKE

*I*t was Saturday and I was sitting at the breakfast bar with Josh. Malinda ducked next door with Nary to borrow some eggs off Mrs Cliff. I made sure as she went out the back door and a brother followed her to and from the place. Josh was telling me about how awesome the new game I bought him was. I'd been going past a gaming store last night and remembered Josh, for the past week, had been going on and on about how all his friends had it but he didn't and he wished he did. So I got it, brought it home and that was when I found out why he shouldn't have had it. Apparently, it was too violent. Malinda had kicked up a stink about it, and when I told her to cool her jets, she didn't like it and stomped off to our room. I sent the kids next door for a bit and went after her of course, she was fuckin' hot when she got riled up.

She turned to me when I walked through the door and glared. Her glare deepened when she caught my lips twitching, I was fighting my smile big time. I explained to her Josh would have seen worse on the TV than what was in the game I'd given him. Plus, the game stated fifteen years and above. Josh turned fifteen in six months. However, when that didn't warm her up, I went on saying that it was the first thing I'd bought him, all his friends had that game and I didn't want him missing out… which was somewhat true. When I saw her eyes melt, I knew the fight was over. The sex after it was fucking brilliant.

Still, now I wished to Christ I hadn't given it to him. There were only so many times I wanted to hear about it, this being the sixtieth fucking time, I was more than over it.

So when there was a knock on the front door, I was eager to get outta the kitchen, but when I opened the door, I would have preferred to listen to Josh going on about that damn game another one hundred times than deal with the person standing on the front stoop.

Helen Delray, my ex, stood with her hands at her sides and a small smile upon her face. With her blonde hair tied up, she wore black slacks and a cream-coloured girly shirt.

Glancing over her shoulder, I eyeballed Dive and Billy. They shrugged and went back to their posts. I'd kill them later for letting her even come to the front door of my woman's house.

"What're you doin' here?" I hissed.

"I heard you moved. I need to talk, Stoke."

"I don't have time or wanna hear what you've gotta say."

"Please," she begged. She looked lost, sad and annoyed all at the same time. I wondered if her visit had anything to do with Ivy, which was why I let her walk through the door.

I gestured to the couch. She walked over, looking around the joint and sat down. I placed myself at the other end of the couch.

"Stoke?" I heard Josh ask.

I looked over my shoulder and said, "Give us some time, kid."

He glared at Helen, but nodded and left the room, heading toward the hallway.

"Who was that?" Helen asked.

I turned my attention to her and said, "None of your business. Say whatever you have to say."

She took a breath and I looked down to her hands fidgeting on her lap. She was nervous, I couldn't help but wonder why.

She licked her lips, looked up to meet my gaze and said, "I wanted to apologise for the way I left things—"

I held up my hand and demanded, "Wait, this has nothing to do with Ivy?"

She bit her bottom lip, a trait I used to like—not anymore—and shook her head.

"Then I don't want to hear it," I said and made a move to

get up, until she placed her hand on mine and said, "Please just hear me out."

I shouldn't have sat back down.

I should've known as lightning outside lit the sky that it was an omen, shit was about to go down.

I didn't listen to myself.

I was a curious fucker.

"Thank you," she said and smiled. "Like I said, I wanted to apologise for the way I was with you. I was scared because you had me feeling things I shouldn't have."

"Yet you fucked that idiot," I said in a bored tone. "What, he didn't give it to you as good as I could, so you want me back?"

"Truth?" she asked. I just stared at her. "I was scared being with a biker would look bad for my career. So to ruin the only good thing I had, I slept with someone I shouldn't have and made sure you caught me. However, doing so not only broke us up, it also caused a rift in mine and Ivy's relationship."

"Because she didn't know what a bitch you really were."

"Yes. I acted out and I made a huge mistake, Stoke. I want you back. I still care deeply for you. I think of you all the time...." she looked down to her lap shaking her head.

"You need to get out now," Josh yelled as he came around the corner of the hall. "Get out," he screamed.

"Kid," I growled.

"No, don't. I saw you were thinking about it. You were thinking of leaving us, all because of her. She needs to leave," he shouted, standing on the other side of the couch with his hands at his side, his fists clenched into tight balls.

I got up and walked around to him, placing my hands on his shoulders, but he backed out of my touch and glared up at me with unshed tears in his eyes.

Fuck.

He'd been listening that whole time.

"Josh," I said in a calm tone.

"Don't." He sniffed. "You should go before Mum gets home, before Nary gets here and you make us all upset. Leave with your whore. Leave us... me," he screamed as tears fell from his eyes onto his red cheeks.

"I— oh, God, Stoke, who is he?"

"The better question is who are you and why does my son look like his new game is broken?" I turned to see Malinda in the kitchen doorway with Nary at her side.

"I'm Helen, Ivy's friend and Stoke's girlfriend."

Malinda sucked in a breath. Nary covered her mouth and grabbed her mum's hand.

"He's leavin' us. He didn't want us. He doesn't like us, Mum," Josh said and then looked to me and added, "I liked you. From the first time, you were different... I thought you cared about us. I thought... you'd never leave. But I'm not good enough. I never am," he uttered, his chin touched his chest and, fuck, my heart just bled.

"Josh," Malinda sobbed. I looked to her, and then to Nary, who both had tears falling down their cheeks.

"Kid," I said in a pained voice and stepped up to him, he backed up.

"Stoke?" Helen called.

"Shut-up," I growled. I didn't have time for her. Maybe I should have kicked her arse out, but I didn't want to waste my breath. She'd soon get the picture. I reached out an arm, tagged Josh's tee at the front and pulled. He stumbled forward into my arms. He tried to break free but I held tight, my arms surrounding his shoulders. I leaned down and told him the truth.

"Listen, kid and do it good. I ain't goin' anywhere. No one will drive me off. You are stuck with me for the long haul. There may be situations like this or fights your mum and I will have that may put doubt in your mind, but don't let it sink in, Josh. I haven't been this happy in a long fuckin' time. Because of you, Nary and your mum, I can finally be happy. I like what we have here. I care about what we have. Nothin' will drag me away, kid. I love your mum. I love you and Nary, just like you were my own. Fuck, it may be too soon to say that, but it's the goddamn truth. I'm staying. The woman got her wires crossed, there is no way in hell I would give any of you up for anythin'."

I shook his shoulders. Halfway through my speech, he'd reached up and grabbed a hold of my tee. "You hear me, kid?" I asked. He nodded against my chest. "You feel me, Josh? You get it, yeah? I ain't goin' anywhere. I love this family." Again, he nodded. "I gotta hear words, kid. Give 'em to me."

He pulled back and looked up at me with red puffy eyes. "I hear you, Stoke. I love ya, too."

"Good," I stated and looked over my shoulder to see Helen standing there crying. "You need to leave and don't ever come back."

She nodded and walked to the door on shaky feet. Before she opened it, she turned and looked to Malinda.

"I'm sorry, so sorry about this. I didn't know Stoke was involved." A sob broke through her. "Ivy, she doesn't talk to me much anymore, and when I asked a biker where Stoke was, he said he moved. He didn't tell me he moved in with you and your family." She wiped her eyes. "If I had known, I wouldn't have come. I would never have come and done this. I can only hope you believe me." With that, she opened the door and left.

Turning my head, I looked to Malinda who had soft eyes for me, and then to Josh and Nary who was still crying. I ordered, "Come here, both of you."

They did. I opened one arm wide. My woman went for the middle, placing an arm around each of her kids. Nary went for my other arm and when they were in, I circled my arms around the lot of them.

Malinda looked up, beaming at me. "You love us?"

With an eye roll and a lip twitch, I said, "Course. Or else I would've been outta here when you both went through your rags together and became total bitches."

"Declan," Malinda snapped.

"Stoke," Nary gasped and punched me in the ribs.

Josh burst out laughing.

"Kids, head next door, your mum and I gotta consummate our love."

"Declan Stoke," Malinda growled.

"What? It's true and they gotta know we do each other."

Nary backed up, pretending to gag. Josh took off down the hall like he was the Flash reincarnated.

As Nary followed her brother, I took my woman in my

arms and looked down into her warm eyes. "I fuckin' love you, Malinda May."

Tears filled her eyes and she pecked my lips. "I love you, too, Declan Stoke. But never talk about us doing each other in front of the kids."

Chuckling I said, "Okay, we'll just do it… later."

"Done." She smiled. "It was fantastic what you did for Josh."

"Nothin' fantastic about the truth, woman. I mean it. You ain't getting rid of me."

"Damn," she giggled. I slapped her arse and ordered, "Bitch, get in that kitchen and cook me some breakfast."

"So rude and annoying, why do I put up with you?"

"Because I make you come every night."

She rolled her eyes. "Well, I suppose there is that."

After she walked into the kitchen, I stood in the living room for a moment to myself.

That was fucking close. I nearly lost the only good in my life.

My chest constricted. I rubbed it.

There was no way I would let that happen again.

I was gonna have to talk to Ivy. I didn't want my woman or kids to have to see Helen's face again and be reminded of the pain they felt in that moment.

In other words, Helen was gonna be banned from showing her face in the club again.

Even if she was sorry. Even if she didn't know any better.

I'd do anything for the people in this house, in my life and in my heart.

Walking to the hall, I yelled down it, "It's safe to come out. We're doin' each other later."

"Declan Stoke," Malinda growled from the kitchen.

Josh yelled back, "TMI, man."

And Nary screamed, "I don't want to know. You guys are sick and old."

Thing was, I heard the humour in all their voices.

CHAPTER EIGHTEEN

TWO MONTHS LATER

MALINDA

*I*t was nearly Christmas and things were blissful. Although, no one still knew where Oscar was, things had settled into an easy medium. I had to get on with my life instead of worrying every day, so I did. I went out with the pussy posse. I visited their homes and got to know all of them more each day. Even though, those outings and visits included guards, I didn't mind. I stopped worrying I was wasting their time. I stopped stressing over if my situation was a pain to them. I had to stop because I had been driving the men crazy with all the panic. Talon even came to my house one day and told me to fuckin' get over it, that they kept their Hawks' members safe. He reassured me he had more than enough men to take it in turns to have our backs and they enjoyed doing it because they wanted me and the children safe. Not only for us, but for their brother, Stoke's, peace of mind. Talon was scary enough to not argue the point with, so I didn't, and got over it all.

Besides, he said if I didn't, he'd send Griz next time and I was scared of him more.

"You ready?" Declan asked from the driver's side of his pick-up. We were about to enter Nancy's house. The children had finished school three weeks ago and Nancy was putting on a party to celebrate Josie graduating high school and the fact she would soon be leaving home, and town, to move to Melbourne to study at one of the biggest university's there, Swinburne.

I was proud and nervous for my daughter going into year twelve, so this was also a celebration for Nary getting good grades and for Saxon, who sat in the back of the car in one corner beside Josh.

Saxon didn't want to come, but he had no choice when we turned up at the compound and I sent Stoke in to get him. He wouldn't dare not listen to Stoke. He admired him too much. So, even with his scowl and grumbling, he got into the pick-up.

I turned in the car seat and looked at the children in the back. Smiling, I asked, "Are you guys ready for some fun?"

Nary nodded, Josh yelled, "Hell yeah."

Saxon asked, "How can a family lunch be fun?"

When I caught Declan's eyes, we both burst out laughing. "Honey," I said to Saxon. "Just wait until you meet

Nancy and Julian." I knew for a fact Saxon hadn't met Julian
as yet, because Julian had a new job, instead of his regular
one as a masseuse. He worked during the day at Talon's
strip club in Geelong where he taught the strippers...or
exotic dancers as Julian called them, new dance moves.

As for Nancy, apparently, Talon had banned her from
the compound for a year because his men were sick of her
babying them or flirting with them.

Climbing out of the pick-up with my bowlful of maca-
roni and cheese pasta salad, I heard the front door open.
Looking up, I spotted Ivy smiling and coming down the
walk.

"Hey, hi, how's it going? Need a hand with anything?"
She waved, grinned and blushed.

Ever since the night at the club when Declan and I
watched Ivy and Killer going at it, she's never been able to
not blush around us. I found it cute and funny. She came to
our house the next day after that night with hands full of
chocolate and DVDs. As soon as I opened the door and saw
her worried face, I reassured her with a warm smile and
invited her in.

Stoke had been out with the children and three other
bikers. I was home alone...well, to the extent of having my
usual guard's front and back.

She got through the door, took a breath and said, "I'm so
sorry. I didn't know the guys had that planned. I mean I did,
but not until, like probably before my man...um, when he,
went down there and you know, by then, I was so turned on I
couldn't think, and then, thinking people were watching,

well... I kinda, liked that thought to, which makes me weird I know. It's like I like showing people the wonderfulness of Fox and me together. I'd never want to be with anyone else or have anyone touch Fox. I would have to hurt someone if they even tried and that would be bad. I hate hurting people, but if some skank came at my man, I'd have claws the size of wolverines."

She started pacing, shaking her head, only to stop abruptly and turned to me where I stood near the front door still. Thankfully, it was closed. "I'm sorry you were put in that position. It was wrong of them and so wrong of me, for... um, not doing anything to stop it. I feel so bad now. Fox said I was being stupid. Apparently, he spoke to Stoke and Stoke told him you didn't mind... that, ah, oh, God, that you liked watching, but I couldn't believe it. I had to come talk to you and see if you hated me for it. I won't let it ever happen again, so you don't need to worry, but I kind of don't want the others to know... that was, you know, um... private."

She threw her hands up in the air and stalked to the couch, placed her items on the coffee table, sat down and said to the floor. "I feel really bad about it all and I guess, I mean, I understand if you don't want to see me or Fox ever again."

I waited.

And waited some more just in case she hadn't finished.

When I thought enough time had passed, I walked to the couch and sat down next to her.

That was when I couldn't keep it in anymore.

I burst out laughing. Her head snapped up and she gaped

at me as I pitched over holding my stomach while I laughed so hard.

"Malinda?"

"Sorry," I said, waving my hand around. "Oh, God, sorry. But that was awesome." I took a deep breath to still my laughter and sat straight looking at Ivy. "Honey, I've heard you chatter before, but… wow, that speech you just delivered was epic." I smiled to show I was teasing. She giggled. "And to reply—Fox was right. It was awkward to start with, but I couldn't take my eyes away from it." It was my turn to blush.

"Really?" she asked.

"Yeah, Ivy." I nodded. "There is nothing wrong with you liking that sort of thing, hell, if anything, I understand it now, more than I ever would. It was erotic and it was lucky I had Declan with me." I giggled and she joined in.

"So… you didn't mind?"

"No, not at all. I've heard people go to special clubs for that sort of thing."

She nodded. "And, you, I mean, ah, you don't feel funny now? With me in your house, after what you saw?"

"I thought maybe I would, but no."

"That's cool." She grinned.

"Yeah, it is." I smiled and then watched a thought cross her face. I had an inkling of what it was, I also knew she wouldn't voice it. She wasn't comfortable, which I found amusing. "Ivy?"

"Yes?" she asked, meeting my gaze.

"Maybe one time the guys would like to do it again… is that weird?"

She blushed and her small grin was sweet, in a shy way. "I think they would like that."

"Good, now let's eat the chocolate before the children get back and see it," I said, standing and heading to the kitchen. "Do you want a coffee to go with it?"

"Yes, please. Mally?"

"Hmm?" I asked and turned to face her.

"You don't mind keeping this just between us?"

Smiling, I said, "I prefer it that way also."

I had been surprised with how blasé I was about it all. Then I thought... I'd never tried different things. My sex life had been sheltered. I liked what Declan and I had. He was bringing my inner hussy forward and I was enjoying it. I think it also had to do with the fact I felt safe around them all. Ivy was an amazing person and I felt the same way she did with Fox. I didn't want anyone touching my man and really... I wouldn't feel right to watch or maybe have someone watch me other than Ivy and Fox. We knew where we both stood. We knew it was private and we knew each partner was off limits.

It couldn't be better.

Later that night when I was in bed with Declan, I told him about Ivy's visit. He rolled on top of me and asked, "So you'd wanna do that again?"

Biting my bottom lip, I shrugged.

"Love, we have to be honest with each other. Would you want to watch Killer and Ivy go at it again?"

"Um... yes." I blushed. He smirked and chuckled. "But, only if you want to?"

"Malinda, I don't give a fuck. If it turns you on, then shit,

193

yes, we're doing it again. If you didn't feel comfortable about it, then we wouldn't bother. But hell, woman, you're always amazing in bed, though, that night, you were on fire."

"So were you." I smiled.

"You be up for doing it with all of us in the same room?"

"I-I'm not sure."

'S'all good. I'd love to show Killer what I have warming my bed every night, but we'll see if it happens. No stress, just go with the flow and see." He touched his lips to my neck, pulled back with heated eyes burning me and growled, "Now, I gotta have you again. My dick is hard for his pussy. You willing to take it again?"

"I'm always willing for you."

"Damn right," he said and kissed me while sliding his hard cock into my already drenched pussy.

I shook my head from all thoughts and focused on Ivy standing in front of me, waiting for an order. "Honey, can you get the chops I brought out of the back?"

"Sure can." She made her way to the back of the pick-up. I watched as Stoke made it there first and undid the tarp. He said something that made her laugh. I thought jealousy would have settled in my stomach, but it didn't.

"Mum, I'm taking Saxon in to meet Nancy," Josh yelled and dragged Saxon down the walk, where Killer was coming up. I nodded, my mind still thinking of other thing, but I saw Nary slowly follow the other two into the house.

Looking back at Ivy and Declan smiling and talking, I wondered again why I didn't feel worry or jealousy over it. Why my claws didn't pop out and why I didn't want to punch Ivy in the face when she gently smacked my man on the chest because, no doubt, he would have said something crude.

"You got a connection with my woman, that's why," Killer said at my back. I glanced over my shoulder at him, my brows drawn up in confusion. He smirked and gestured with his chin to our partners. "It's why right now I won't go over and gut my brother for teasing my woman in a way I don't usually like. Stoke and I have a connection. He's the only one I talk to, the main one I reach out to more than the others. He's my family, my brother in more ways than the patch on our vests.

"I know he's only foolin' around. He means nothing by what he does with or to Ivy. I know because he talks about you constantly, drives me fuckin' crazy, but it shows me he loves you. What we shared, that time you watched us," I blushed, and he chuckled, "that just deepened the connection, to share something so private like that. Ivy has a big heart, and she's warmed to you more than the others. You and her have the same connection Stoke and I have. It's how what we do in private won't wreck what we already have."

Ivy gasped at something Declan said and yelled, "Shut-up, Stoke." I laughed at them. Killer was right. There was a connection between the four of us and that connection was special.

I turned to Killer and said, "You're right and it's awesome."

His lips twitched, he replied with a smug, "I know."

Rolling my eyes, I said, "Whatever, why don't you make

yourself useful, go help them grab some stuff from the back."

Laughing, he walked off. I glanced at the three of them, my heart jumped and started into a beautiful beat. I liked what I had. No, I loved what I had with these people, especially my man. He was amazing in many ways. Even if he was sometimes demanding, annoying and possessive. I wouldn't want what we have with anyone else.

"Come on, people, get your butts moving," I called to them.

All three looked at me and smiled. Stoke also added a wink. It was then I knew I wanted to have another private viewing and soon.

CHAPTER NINETEEN

STOKE

*W*atching Malinda across the big yard was warming my chest. She sat on a huge-arse blanket on the ground with the younger kids. Swan was reading her something while Drake and Ruby were sitting and listening, while playing with some toys. She looked great. She looked right. She needed my seed planted in her to pop out our own tribe of little people.

Even though babies scared the fuck outta me, in a way that made my palms sweat, I'd still do it. Hell, I'd known for a long time I wanted Malinda May knocked up. She'd look fucking awesome big with my kid inside her. Besides, my woman was the one who had to feed them and change them. I hoped to Christ anyway.

Turning back to Talon, I asked, "Any updates?"

Shaking his head, he said, "Nah, brother. It's like he's fuckin' vanished into thin air."

"Anthony wouldn't be playin' us, would he? Maybe he's got Oscar hold up somewhere or some shit," Griz mentioned.

"I spoke to Anthony this mornin'," Killer said. We all turned to him.

"What the fuck do you mean you spoke to him?" I demanded.

He shrugged. "No one is getting anything. We needed all our eyes after Oscar and not worried about Anthony making a move, so I talked to him."

"You went in on your own? Didn't you think to mention any of this shit to us?" Talon growled.

"It was nothin'. Besides, Stoke would have done the same for me."

"I don't want shit hung over your head for anything, Killer; you're just gettin' your life back," I snapped. "You imagine if I had to go to Ivy one day and say her man was dead because of some shit he did for me." I shook my head. "That is something I never wanna do."

"You won't have to, fucker," Killer growled.

"Dude, just say what you mean so we can all chill again," Blue offered. Our group had gone from laid back to tense in seconds.

I shifted on my feet, took a pull from my beer and glared at Killer, waiting for his answer.

"Three years ago, Anthony called me up and asked me for a favour. I did it; he owed me one. So I called in the return favour, now he's not gonna do shit to Malinda or her kids. He's waiting for Oscar to show himself. He doesn't have him, but if we get him first, he wants us to give him over."

The tightness in my chest eased and I looked to Talon.

"Your call, brother. What do you want to do with Oscar if we get him first?"

Fuck. What I wanted to do was make the motherfucker pay.

Killer had taken this risk for my woman's safety and there was no way in hell I'd want anything to happen to her, him or Ivy.

"Talk to him about my feelin's, then hand him over."

Talon, Griz and Blue chuckled. They knew exactly what I meant. I looked to Killer who was smirking.

"Thanks, brother."

"Any-fuckin'-time."

Richard, Zara's dad, stepped up to the fold and said, "So, tell me what in the hell is happening about finishing Malinda's troubles?"

"We got it covered, Rich," Talon said.

"Covered? Is that what you call it? Why back in my day, I'd be busting down doors and threatening people. You done that yet?"

My lips twitched and fuck, mine weren't the only ones. I wasn't sure how many doors Rich had busted down in his days, but I would have loved to have been a fly on the wall. I was sure my brothers were thinking the same thing.

"Don't worry, Rich, I busted down three just yesterday," Blue grinned.

Rich studied him, glared and said, "You're pulling my leg.

You're damn lucky, Blue, you're a nice man for our Clary, or I'd have to take you out for being a wise arse."

That was the great thing about Nancy and Rich. Zara wasn't their only child. Whoever Zara or Mattie called their family, so did Nancy and Rich. They'd take anyone into their hearts with open arms.

"Excuse me," Nancy called from the back steps that led into their four-bedroom brick home. "I'd just like to say something please."

A few groans were let free; the loudest one was from her husband.

"Shut-up, Richard, and get up here."

"Jesus. Wish me luck, boys."

We all laughed as he slowly, just to piss Nancy off, made his way to stand at his wife's side. Everyone knew he was full of shit. He loved his wife like it was the first day they married. He loved teasing her even more.

"Okay, Richard and I would like to say a thank you to everyone coming today." Crap, tears welled in her eyes already. "Our beautiful Josie girl has done us so proud," she gushed, looking down at her adopted daughter who was sitting in a group with Zara, Nary and Malinda. "She has blossomed into a gorgeous woman all too soon. Now she is moving out of our nest and taking on the world. It doesn't seem like it's only been two years with you, baby girl. It seems like you have lived with us all along. We have cherished each day we've had with you in our home. You, my dear Josie, are our daughter—"

"Suffer," Rich added, causing everyone to laugh.

"You have a family who will be here for you any time

you need us. We wish you well and a safe journey in your next step in life—"

"Goddamn it woman, stop droning on," Rich said, Nancy punched him, but laughed, then she turned and sobbed into Rich's chest. "Shit," Rich said and wiped his own eyes. "Josie, all you need to know, girl, is we love you. We're very proud, call on us any time while you're away. We know it isn't far, even if Nancy is making out it's like a world away. We're here for you, yeah? Oh, and don't forget us when you're bringing in the money." He laughed to cover his real feelings.

Everyone watched as Josie, with tears falling down her face, got up and walked over to embrace her parents.

I wasn't sure if anyone else noticed. But I sure did, and it had me wondering what the fuck was going on.

Over near the side gate entrance stood a fuming Pick. He looked pissed, but he also looked sad. The plastic cup he had in his hand crinkled under his grip. He looked down at it glaring, then he threw it to his side before he stormed out the gate.

Did Pick have a thing for Josie?

It made sense to his reaction about her leaving.

It was also known Billy had a thing for Josie, she had one for him ever since he carried her from her Hell and into the hospital.

Fuck it.

I was confused and it was none of my business.

Unless one of them came to me.

"What the hell is up with Pick and Billy?" Griz asked. He

gave a chin lift toward the side gate where I saw Billy walking out of it.

"I think it best we stay outta that one," Blue said.

"Apparently, they both have a thing for Josie, but she can't choose between the two of them, so she's not picking either one. Another reason she's moving away. However, the boys are also keeping their distance because she's only eighteen and inexperienced. She's shy as shit and skittish still. Not so much around them, still, she has her moments," Talon said, we all stared at him with shock.

"Jesus," he snarled. "The women fuckin' talk. It's not like I look to know this shit, then there's also the fact my wife is her sister and I'm stuck with Nancy as a mother-in-law."

"Boss, it's kinda scary with how much you do know," Griz said. We all busted out laughing.

"Motherfuckers," Talon growled. How in the hell did my woman find Talon and Griz two of the most scary bastards she knew I wouldn't know.

Then again. When they both went through their own shit with their women, anyone could see the demon they fought inside of themselves to get their women back safe.

They were badarses when it came to their families. Even Blue and Killer had showed their own demons when it came to Clary and Ivy.

It was something I finally understood.

CHAPTER TWENTY

TWO DAYS LATER

STOKE

Malinda was sitting next to me in my pick-up, her hands in her lap, ringing them against each other. She was nervous; shit, anyone could see it from just one look at her. Her eyes were wide and she was biting that sweet bottom lip while constantly fidgeting.

I reached over and took her hand in mine. She glanced at me and gave me a small smile. "I can't help it," she said.

"If it doesn't happen, it doesn't happen. No need to stress about it, love," I reassured her. She nodded and went back to staring out the front window. We were on our way over to Ivy and Killer's. The kids were staying at Mrs Cliff's and we were in for a night of drinking and fooling around. I didn't care if we didn't get to the fooling around part. I was happy to just go there, shoot the shit and drink Killer under the table. It had been Ivy and Malinda's idea. Killer and I just went along with it. Our women got off from porno shit. I was happy and fuckin' horny just doing anything with Malinda. Her gorgeous body still drove me crazy every day and she was a maniac in bed. Couldn't get enough. It was only last night she admitted she'd never been this adventures in bed, that I brought out the bad in her, and fuck I was glad for it.

"Love, seriously, stop fuckin' stressin'. You know Killer and I don't care either way. We get off on our partners no matter. Hell, I could come in my jeans now from just lookin' at your boobs in that goddamn sexy dress."

She giggled. "Thanks and I know. Ivy and I know, but we do want to do this. I can't help but get nervous. They'll see my body for the first time."

"What the fuck, babe. You're worried about that? Shit, woman, if you didn't see it the first time, the only person that will really be seein' it is Ivy. I only have eyes for you and Killer only has eyes for his woman. We don't share. He doesn't touch you because he knows if he tried, I'd kill him, and fuck, vice versa. So don't worry, yeah?"

"Really?"

"Really what, Malinda?"

"You only have eyes for me?"

"Fuck, yes. Don't get me wrong, Ivy is hot, but since you came along, my dick only grows hard for you… every-fuckin'-time you walk into a room for God's sake."

She laughed again, leaned over and kissed my cheek. "Thanks, handsome. I feel a heap better now."

"Good, 'cause we're here." I smiled.

We climbed outta the car and my woman loaded my arms up with grocery bags. The women had organised that Ivy would get the booze and we had to bring all the munchies. But ten fucking bags of munchies was going overboard.

That thought I kept to myself. I didn't want to start shit before we walked in. See, I was learning.

Killer opened the door after I kicked it. Hey, my fucking hands were full. He took one look and said, "What the fuck? Are you feedin' an army?"

Malinda growled a cute growl and pushed past Killer who was smirking down at her. "Shut-it, killjoy," Malinda snapped. She'd taken to calling my brother Killjoy when he wouldn't let Ivy out to watch *Fifty Shades of Grey*, some porn movie, because she'd be too busy fucking him. Malinda sputtered over the phone and yelled, 'Killjoy,' and hung up.

Two days later, our women, with Zara, Dee, Julian, and Clary went and saw the movie, and for some reason, my woman came home with a blush on her face and a huge smile.

"Yo, brother." Killer smirked.

"S'up?" I asked.

"Ready to have a drink. You?"

"Shit, yeah." I grinned and headed down the hall to the kitchen.

"Look out," Ivy yelled just as her dog Trixie came running around the corner and jumped on me. With my hands full, I went off balance and fell on my arse. Killer busted his arse laughing as Trixie then continued to lick my face.

I WAS SITTING on one couch in the living room with my woman and across from us was Killer and Ivy. We were talking about random shit. For Killer and me, it was regarding work. Ivy was dribbling on about some book she was reading and suggesting it to Malinda. We'd had a few drinks, as in Malinda and Ivy we're looking way too happy, and Killer and I were just in a relaxed state.

Out the corner of my eye, I saw Ivy wink at my woman. She then leaned into Killer and whispered something in his ear.

"Woman," Killer growled deeply. He turned to her. She laughed and tried to make an escape. He grabbed her wrist, pulled her down onto the couch where he lay on top of her and took her mouth. She moaned around his lips and wrapped her arms around his neck.

Looking to my woman, she glanced at me with big eyes and then started giggling.

It wasn't a giggling matter. I took her upper arm and tugged her over to me. She landed facing me on my lap, her legs on each side of my hips. "What you laughing about, love?" I smirked up at her. Already my dick was growing hard. The only thing separating us were her panties and my jeans. Her dress was billowed out around my legs.

She licked her lips. All humour died from her face. "Deck."

"Yeah, love?" I asked, running my hands up and down her sides.

She placed her hands on my shoulders, leaned in so her gorgeous breasts pressed against my chest and uttered, "Kiss me."

I did. I claimed her mouth with mine. Her hands left my shoulders and wound around my neck. With my hands on her hips, I ground her down onto my cock, and both of us broke from the kiss to moan.

It was then my woman took over. She pushed down hard against my erection and rubbed her pussy over me, back and forth, back and forth.

My dick was still wanting more. It was begging for freedom. Not yet, I commanded it. While my woman was grinding down on me, I slid one hand under her dress. She looked over her shoulder to see Killer was already working at pleasuring his woman. He was still on top of her with a hand between her legs. Ivy's heated stare met my woman's and they shared a smile.

But when my fingers moved Malinda's panties aside and touched her clit, her head swivelled back to me and I smiled. She gave me a sultry smile and continued driving my cock crazy as she dry humped me.

Though, I wouldn't be dry for long. My woman was soaking.

LILA ROSE

MALINDA

My man was the centre of my attention, what Ivy and Killer were doing was like background music to me. The noises, moans and cries were like an extra hit of adrenalin to the thrill I was already feeling for Declan.

I was riding his fingers now as we kissed roughly and eagerly. Then all of a sudden, he stopped. His hands went back to my waist and next, I was standing in front of him.

Looking up at with wild hooded eyes, he licked his lips and reached up under my dress and slowly, oh so bloody slowly, he pulled my soaked panties down my thighs, over my knees, my calves and then he let them go at my feet.

"Fox, God," With a quick glance over my shoulder I saw Ivy and Killer had advanced from their last position. Ivy had her back to the couch laying on her side. Killer was laying in front of her on his side as well, only their heads were at opposite ends. Ivy's skirt was bunched up; she had one leg bent, her foot to the couch and Killer was between her legs. Down the other end, Ivy, with half-mast eyes, full with desire, was bobbing her head up and down. She was sucking on Killer's cock fast, and she was loving it.

My gaze went back to my man as he glided his finger up the sides of my legs. When his hands came to my hips, they stopped. I leaned over. I knew what I wanted. I only hoped Declan wouldn't mind. As I kissed him, I undid his jeans, tugged them open and pulled his cock free from its confinements.

He hissed as I ran my hand up and down his length. He broke the kiss to throw his head back against the couch,

208

closed his eyes and grunted out a groan. Then, "Jesus, love," he uttered.

Suddenly, his eyes opened, he leaned forward, tagged my hips and pulled. My knees landed on each side of his waist, he pushed my arse up, lined his cock up with my pussy hole and then pushed me down, embedding myself fully onto his thick dick.

Moaning, he ran his hands up my back then he pulled me forward and our mouths touched, opened and fought. All the while, I lifted myself up and down on my man's hardness.

Forcing us apart so I could breathe, my head still went back further. I looked to the ceiling and gasped.

God, it felt so good.

"Christ." I heard Killer groan. I looked around. They were kneeling on the couch, Ivy in front of Killer, her stomach against the back of the couch and Killer was right behind her, his hips thrusting back and forth. He was fucking his woman.

I looked back down to my man. His head was back against the couch, his eyes closed tightly; he was close.

Touching my mouth to his, his eyes opened. He smiled up at me as I slid up and down faster on him.

"You feel so good in me," I uttered.

"It's where I'm supposed to be... fuck, always."

"Yes," I moaned. "God, I'm close, handsome."

"Let me bring you there, love," he growled.

Behind us, Ivy's cry of release and Killer's grunt filled the room. They had finished, their breathing erratic. Just hearing it, knowing they had both reached their end was something erotic and caused me to bite my lower lip.

Declan's hand slid under my dress. He knew my weakness when I had him inside me. It never took me long once he was inside and he touch my clit.

"God, yes!" Just like that. His thumb ran up and down over my swollen nub. My head fell back and I closed my eyes tightly as a climax ripped through me.

As my inner walls tightened around my man's cock, I felt him swell within me, next, he clutched my hair in his fist, forced my mouth down to his and he kissed me as he pumped his seed inside of me.

The whole scene was wild, hot and fun. Experiencing the bliss with other people in the room made it intense. It was a secret worth keeping… and worth doing again.

CHAPTER TWENTY-ONE

MALINDA

*W*aking up the next day smiling told me how much I enjoyed the previous night, especially when we got home and had a bath together. I'd never had water sex before, it was definitely something I wanted to do again.

Declan was still sound asleep next to me with his arm slung over my waist. He looked amazing in the morning light that managed to seep in through the curtains. His fohawk haircut was ruffled, making him look younger than usual. I was reluctant to move, but I had to. Looking at the alarm clock on the bedside, which read ten am, we were getting a delivery soon from the grocery store.

Crawling quietly out of bed, I put on my robe. The morning must have been cold because as soon as my feet touched the hard wood floor, they cringed at the freshness. Donning a pair of fluffy slippers, I walked to the adjoining bathroom and did my morning ritual.

As I made my way into the kitchen dressed in jeans and a jumper, I thought and hoped that Mrs Cliff was able to get the children off to school on time. Though, they were getting a lift with Saxon, so I knew the possibility was high because he wouldn't put up with them delaying him.

I went and placed water in the kettle and switched in on. As I waited for it to boil, I looked out the kitchen window and thought of last night. What we'd done at Ivy's was hot, sexy and so goddamn thrilling. It was something that could only happen every now and then, because of our hectic lives. I also knew what we were doing wasn't going to last forever, and I was happy with that. It was as though it was a stage we were going through together, a stage we all enjoyed and thought was fun while it lasted.

Nothing lasted forever.

Except... my love for my man.

After our bath escapade, Declan had taken me to bed and had me again. However, the way he moved over me felt different from all times before. It was as though he was cherishing my body in a new way. The sweet, soft ways he touched me and slid his cock into me was wonderful. Just thinking of it made me giddy with excitement and love.

The whistle to the kettle made me jump and then the knock at the front door caused me to squeal. Walking quickly out into the living room, I spotted Declan coming down the hall wearing only jeans. I was never one to stop and admire the scenery, but that time, I did. My feet screeched to a stop and I eyed my man as he strutted his large, amazing form my way with a smirk upon his face.

"Love, you can devour me later. Right now, I need to get the door." He chuckled as he strode past me and slapped me on the butt. He flung the door open, and standing on the other side was a teenage boy with a pimply face, holding a box of groceries. "Thanks," Declan said.

The boy's eyes widened. Oh, he must be new to the job. He looked scared of Declan and I could understand why. He was a huge man with scars on his chest and stomach.

"I-I-I'll just g-get the other box," the poor boy stuttered, then turned and bolted down the path to his running van.

Walking up behind Declan as he placed the first box on the floor inside the house, I slid my arms around his waist. My fingers barely touched because of his wide frame. "You know," I started, "Maybe you should let me answer the door next time. I think you scared the poor boy."

He snorted. "It'd do him good to be scared."

Rolling my eyes, I kissed his back and picked up the box from the floor, taking it to the kitchen.

After placing it on the bench, I went to the kettle once again and turned it on. I grabbed two mugs down and filled Declan's with coffee, while I was in the mood for my favourite cup of tea. I took the tea box from the shelf, but it was empty.

I turned and smiled, thank God, we'd just received a delivery. I couldn't last without a cup of tea. Unpacking the items, I finally found a new box at the bottom just as Stoke came walking into the kitchen with the other box and some grocery bags.

"You're right. I think that kid just peed himself." He smiled and put the stuff down on the bench. He came around the counter and swung me into his arms.

"Well, you are big and scary," I mentioned.

"Maybe it didn't help when Blue and Dive rode up on their rides. He took one look at their vests and then back to me to see me wave, in the next second, there was a wet patch on the front of his jeans."

My hand went to my mouth to cover my laugh. I really shouldn't find that amusing.

"That's mean." I grinned.

"Can't help your man's big and scary. You like it anyway." He scowled down at me and barked, "Get my fuckin' coffee, bitch."

"Pfft, don't you dare try that on me," I snapped half-heartily, kissed his cheek and pushed him back. I went back to finish our drinks. Turning around with my cup in my hand, I watched as my man made his way around the kitchen putting our groceries away.

I blew on my hot tea before saying, "You're my kitchen bitch." Then I burst out laughing when all of a sudden, his body stilled halfway in the fridge with a milk container in his hand.

He blinked and slowly stood straight. "You did not just say that to me."

When my laughter died down, I shrugged and said, "Yeah," then took a sip of my tea. He started for me. "No, you keep doing what you're doing," I ordered. He growled and kept coming. I managed three more sips before he took it from my hand and placed it on the bench behind me.

"You'll pay for that comment, love," he hissed. He spun me around and made me place my hands on the bench in front of me.

I moaned loudly as he ran his hand over my arse, then smacked it. "Declan," I gasped. I gripped the bench tighter as dizziness took me. "Declan," I said in a panicked tone.

"Malinda?" he asked in a worried voice, "You're swaying, love. What's wrong?'

I wanted to answer him, I did, but my mouth felt like it was full of cotton. My legs buckled under me. I would have hit the ground if Declan didn't catch me.

"I... don't... feel... well," I managed to tell him.

"Fuck, love. Malinda, open your eyes for me." I felt a light tap on my cheek.

My eyes are open, aren't they?

No. Oh, God, I can't open my eyes. Help!

"Malinda," my man yelled. "Christ, no, no. Shit."

I felt him pick up my body and walk. I knew I was laid on the couch seconds later; I felt it under my back, but I couldn't do anything. I couldn't move, open my eyes or talk.

What's wrong with me? Why can't I do anything? Wetness touched my cheeks, I knew it was tears from my eyes.

"Blue! Dive!" Declan bellowed. I was surprised the house didn't shake from it. I heard the front door bang open.

"Stoke, what the fuck?"

"She's not waking up, brother." I heard the pain in his voice, the panic. I wanted to reach out and reassure him, still I couldn't. I was pissed I couldn't. I didn't want him to worry.

"Call the paramedics, call Killer," I heard Blue order.

Dive must have walked back outside because I couldn't hear him, but I knew he would be doing as he was asked.

Blue's footfalls came closer, but suddenly, Declan yelled, "Stop. Don't, Jesus, don't go near her."

Oh, God, please let me open my eyes. My man was hurting. I needed to tell him I was okay.

"Stoke, we've got people on the way," Dive said.

"Dive," Blue warned. He must have been coming toward me.

"Back the fuck off," Declan screamed. I felt my body being moved. I was on the floor now, in Declan's warm arms.

"It's all right, brother," Blue said. Something shifted along the floor. Had they moved the couch out of the way?

God, I didn't know. Declan started rocking me in his arms and more fresh tears fell from my closed eyes.

"It's gonna be okay, love. You're gonna be okay," he said over and over.

I wasn't so sure it would be.

The worst of it all, was feeling my man breaking and knowing I couldn't do anything about it.

I was helpless.

Never would I believe my heart would bleed once again after what Tank had done to me.

But it was. It was bleeding...no it was drowning in blood for my man.

STOKE

The pain was unimaginable. The force of it wanted to take me to the ground. No pain had ever been as intense or severe before... fuck, it was agonizing.

"Sir, you have to let us take her," the dweeb ambo guy said in a patronising tone. I wanted to hit him. They arrived only seconds earlier, but I was in no state to do anything. Instead of listening, I rocked my woman in my arms telling her everything would be okay.

"Sir, could she be pregnant?"

No, she couldn't be, right? I didn't know. I knew fucking nothing but pain.

So I didn't answer.

"Sir, let us take her," he said in a forceful tone, reaching out for my woman.

A growl filled the room.

"Fuck, you need to back the fuck up, slowly. I'll deal with it."

"Shit," the ambo guy said and moved away. I was glad he did because I was about to wrap my hand around his throat.

"Stoke," that was Killer. I felt him next to me. "Brother. Your woman needs help. They need to check her over, to fix her," he pleaded. "Stoke, Christ, brother you're doing her no good. Let her go."

"She's crying, Killer. Look, see her tears. How is she crying in her sleep? She's asleep, right?"

"Yeah, brother, it looks like it. But we need to make sure."

I knew the right thing to do was let her go, let them see

what was wrong. But fuck! *Fuck!* I was scared. So scared, more scared than I had been in my life. What happened if I let her go and I never saw her again? They'd take her and I'd never have my soul again.

Right then, she was breathing. She was in my arms safe and breathing.

Everything else hurt.

I didn't know what to think. I didn't want to do anything but hold my woman while she slept.

"I can't let her go, brother," I uttered. "I can't do it. Christ, if I let her go, it will be real. She shouldn't be like this. She won't wake up, Killer. Fuck!" My breath hitched. I felt like a pussy in front of my brothers, but I didn't care. This was my woman, my life and my soul.

I clamped my eyes tight, cleared my throat and said, "You need to take her. You need... take her from me."

"Blue, Dive," Killer said into the room. Footsteps every-where and then I felt heat at my back.

"Jesus," someone hissed.

"All right, brother?" Killer asked and then placed his hand on my woman's arm. My upper lips raised. I didn't like to see it there. "Calm, Stoke. I won't harm her. You know that. I have Ivy, yeah?"

Fuck.

Motherfucking Christ.

He had Ivy. He had a woman. He wasn't taking my life away.

Killer gently tugged on her arm. I growled, "Wait." I put my nose into her hair, near her ear and whispered, "My sweet, Malinda, I need to let you go, but not for long, love.

They'll fix you and I'll be there. I'll be there for you, Malinda, always and forever." I ground my teeth together and took a deep breath. "I love you, Malinda May. Be strong, be strong for both of us. I-I need you. Shit, love, you fight, whatever this is, fight for me, for Josh and Nary, and for our future." Pulling away from her scent killed me. "On three," I hissed.

"Right," Killer said. "One, two, three." In seconds, he had her from my arms and laying on the floor as Blue and Dive grabbed my arms and took me to my stomach on the floor, and I let out a roar of fury.

"Take her out," Killer yelled. I watched from the floor, struggling to break free from my brothers to get to her. "Take him to the car. Follow the ambulance. Now!" he barked.

I was lifted from the floor in a tight, unyielding grip, and dragged from the house.

CHAPTER TWENTY-TWO

NARY

*J*osh was upstairs when I heard the sirens of an ambulance and straight away, I knew something was wrong. I ran from the room leaving Mrs Cliff in the kitchen as she yelled my name. I ignored her.

At the window, I shifted the curtain out of the way. My heart sunk, the ambulance stopped right out the front of my house.

Mum.

Stoke.

No, no no.

"Child, come away from the window," Mrs Cliff said and tugged my arm.

I pulled it from her grip, shaking my head. "I have to go over there."

"You will not. You stay here. They have it under control."

"Please, I have to… I, my mum… no," I cried as I watched paramedics run into the house. Harleys pulled up out the front. Killer, Stoke's best friend, and another biker, Dodge, I think, got off their bikes and ran into the house.

Mrs Cliff turned to the hall as we heard the back door being slammed open. I didn't move my gaze from the house next door. I itched to get over there. I needed to see. I needed to know. She couldn't keep me here… not when something was happening to my mum or Stoke.

"I have to go over there," I hissed through clenched teeth.

My hand went to my chest. My heart was hurting. It was scared, like me.

I can't lose my mum.

I can't.

She's everything to me.

I promise I'll be good, God. I promise I won't give anyone any trouble. I'll get good grades. I'll listen to Mum and Stoke all the time.

I'll be good.

Just help them. Please, don't take them.

"Mrs Cliff," a deep voice said behind me. Still I didn't turn. I didn't care.

"I have to go over there," I uttered, pleading.

"You'll stay here," that same deep voice ordered.

Spinning around, I faced Saxon. "You know what's going on? You know. Oh, God, tell me, please, please tell me." I ran at him and saw him brace. Just stopping before him, I grabbed his tee into my hands and shook. "What's going on?"

"I don't know anything. I was sent here to stay in the house with you and your brother."

"Child, you need to shush before you alert your brother," Mrs Cliff said.

My hand went over my mouth. Tears ran freely down my face, but I caught the sob before it was heard. I closed my eyes. My head falling to Saxon's chest. He stiffened.

I have to be strong for my brother.

Seeing this, hearing this, will kill him.

He's too scared already from the thought of losing either of them.

I have to be strong.

After composing myself, somewhat, I took a deep breath, lifted my head and stepped away from Saxon and his wide eyes.

"You're right, Mrs Cliff. Josh can't know. Hopefully the video games will keep him occupied for hours, like usual," I said with a calm voice, while on the inside I screamed and cried.

Without thinking, my feet took me back to the window. When I saw Stoke being dragged from the house cursing and fighting, I grabbed the curtain.

Next, oh, God, next the paramedics were wheeling my mum out on their trolley.

Please.

No...

"Nary," Saxon said from behind me. His hands land on my shoulders.

'Don't," I ordered. *Please don't or I'll crack.* "Mrs Cliff, I need to know if my brother is still safe here. I need to know what happened so I can prepare him... me."

"Okay, child. I'll find out," she offered sympathetically.

Wiping at my face angrily, I stood at the window and waited and watched.

I watched until there was nothing left to watch.

I watched until the house next-door...our house, fell silent.

And then I prayed some more.

MALINDA

I was in the ambulance on the way to the hospital. My man, my devastated man was in another vehicle. I could hear his screams still in my head. He cursed and fought his brothers to get back to me. To take me. He knew I needed help, but he was scared.

KILLER

"So that guy's her husband?" the medic checking Malinda's vitals asked.

I wasn't in the goddamn mood for stupid questions, still I found myself saying, "Not yet, but he will be."

"I've never seen a guy act like that."

My eyes watched everything he did. Stoke wouldn't want it any other way. I wouldn't let anything harm her when he wasn't there. Finally, I answered the twerp. "She's his life. Without her, he is nothing."

"How do you know?"

I snorted. Frustrated he was so dumb. "Because I'm the same way with my woman," I snapped, then barked, "Enough chit-fuckin'-chat. Do you know what's going on with her?"

"Not yet, but her vitals are fine. It's strange."

"What the fuck is going on?" I voiced my thoughts as I took her hand in mine. "You'd better be okay, Malinda." Fuck, I prayed she was or else I wasn't sure if I could save anyone in Stoke's war path.

Her hand tightened slightly in mine. My eye swung to our hands. "She just gripped my hand," I told him.

"That's great. It's a good sign." He nodded as we came to a stop. The back doors were pulled open and two nurses were there. They helped with the trolley, then wheeled it toward the doors while the medic rattled off her vitals.

"Killer!" My name was bellowed. Turning quickly as Stoke raced toward the doors with his cousin Lan running after him.

"He can't come in this way," the medic who drove said. "You need to control him or he won't see her at all."

Fuck.

Controlling a man when it came to his woman was impossible.

Still, I started for my brother and braced when we collided. Pulling him to the ground, I waited for backup.

Stoke struggled, cursed and fought away from me. His eyes aimed at the door as they closed, with his woman on the other side.

"Stoke, fuck, brother, calm it or they won't let you in," I barked. "Listen to me," I ordered. "Fuckin' listen. She grabbed my hand, brother. She moved. She's going to be okay."

It was then he sagged into my arms and uttered, "Christ."

NARY

"Nary child, come here," Mrs Cliff called from the kitchen. For some reason, I didn't want to move from the window, but I forced myself to. Feeling weary and emotional, I walked down the hall with a quiet Saxon following me. Had he been with me in the living room that whole time? I didn't know, and if he had, I didn't understand it.

On entering, I took a seat opposite Mrs Cliff and looked to her. She smiled and said, "I just spoke to Lan. He's Stoke's cousin and a copper. He said they're at the hospital because your mum collapsed." I gasped. She reached out and grabbed my hand. "It's okay, child. They're running tests. They'll find what's wrong and help your mum."

"B-but what about Stoke? Why were they dragging him out?"

She grinned then. "You mum's man, he didn't like seeing your mum like that. He took it badly. He's at the hospital now with her. Lan said they'd ring once they knew more."

"Sounds like it's gonna be okay," Saxon said from where he stood in the doorway.

I nodded, my eyes to the table. Stoke really cared for mum, the way he was...I had never seen love like that in my life.

Straightening in my seat, I looked up to Mrs Cliff. All I had to do was wait for the next phone call that would inform us Mum was indeed fine. I had to believe. Believing was a good way to go, a good way to live.

A sense of ease settled over me. Yes, all I had to do was believe and put on a brave face for Josh until we knew more.

That was possible.

I thought it was, until a form stepped through the back door.

"No," I gasped.

Mrs Cliff turned in the seat. "The fuck?" she uttered.

Because there stood Malcolm with a gun pointed at us.

"Thought you could get rid of me? Thought that would be the end of it? Have your new daddy threaten mine to send me away. You ruined my life, slut, and now it's time to pay."

"Listen here, you little shit. You leave this child alone and I won't have to hurt you. Get the fuck out of my house," Mrs Cliff warned as she stood.

"Shut it, Grandma, or I'll shoot you first."

"Well, you're gonna have to if you want her."

Malcolm smirked and then laughed. "Easy," he said, aimed his gun and shot Mrs Cliff.

My scream rang throughout the house. Mrs Cliff

gripped the table behind her as she stumbled backward. I was out of my chair in seconds and helped her sink back into her chair. She placed a hand over her breast. Her face was already pale.

"Damn, that hurts more than I remembered." Mrs Cliff cringed.

"Don't talk," I ordered and looked up to a smiling Malcolm. "Let me call an ambulance and then I'll go with you," I pleaded, new tears filling my eyes. I looked for Saxon, but he wasn't there.

"You get nothing. Come here, bitch," he yelled.

"No," I uttered.

"Now!" he bellowed, I jumped. It was then I watched him take a breath. He added, "Come with me now, or I'll shoot her again."

"H-how did you find me?" I asked. Stalling always worked in the movies. I could only hope it worked in this situation.

Malcolm laughed without a trace of humour. "A little friend of your mumma's came to me after my dad had sent me away. All I had to do was poison her tea get her to the hospital and he'd be there to take her, then I got to have you to myself. We'll have so much fun before I kill you."

"You poisoned my mum," I cried.

He shrugged. "Sure and in return, like I said, I got you and fifty thousand dollars."

Without thought, I lunged for him, only I didn't make it. A strong arm wound around my waist. I let out an *ooof* when my advance stopped short.

I was pushed behind a large form, I realised quickly it was Saxon.

"You," Malcolm snarled.

"Why don't you put your gun away and fight like a real man," Saxon barked.

"Yeah, right," Malcolm snorted. "I don't think so."

"You take her... I'll make you regret it."

"See, I don't think you're going to win this time. I have the upper hand here." he shook the gun around. "I think you need to listen to me."

Saxon laughed. He actually laughed, then said, 'I don't think so."

Malcolm aimed once again. I screamed, "No." and lunged for Saxon, knocking him into the wall and then to the floor. The gun went off, then there was silence.

"You havin' fun without us again, Beth?" a gravelly voice asked.

Looking up from the floor, I saw Trevor Boon and Dallas Gan, men I had met one day at Mrs Cliff's. Only it was Dallas restraining a pissed-looking Malcolm.

"Let me go," he roared.

"Not likely," Dallas barked.

"You wanna get off me now, viper?" I looked down at Saxon. Sugar, I'd forgotten I tackled him and was laying on him.

"Do I want you to get me off?" Was that what he said?

Dallas, Trevor and Saxon laughed. I blushed.

Mum.

"Oh, God, we have to call Stoke. Malcolm poisoned

Mum. Oscar's at the hospital waiting for her. He'll take her. We need to warn them. Now!" I stood quickly.

"You're probably too late," Malcolm taunted.

"Calm, child," Mrs Cliff uttered. I looked to her, gasped, and ran to her side to see her flip her phone closed. "I had Lan on the line. He knows. Hopefully, they're dealing with him now." She tried to straighten, I helped her, watching her flinch and wince. She looked to Dallas and Trevor and said, "'Bout time you two idiots got here."

"What you want done with this before we take you to the hospital?" Dallas asked.

"He's mine," Saxon said. He went over to Malcolm and punched him in the stomach. While he was doubled over, Saxon grabbed Malcolm's hair pulled his head up and hissed, "Told you I'd make you pay." He let his head drop and said to Dallas, "Billy will be here soon. He'll take him to the compound."

It was then Josh came running into the kitchen and said, "I'm starving, that game is freakin' awesome. I swear even with the headphones on the gun shots sounded like it was happening in the house." He stopped looked about and uttered, "Oh, shit."

CHAPTER TWENTY-THREE

MALINDA

*M*y body was tingling. I could feel more, but my eyes still wouldn't open or my mouth wouldn't scream what I wanted to say. My man needed me.

"Take her to the end room," a female voice said. The trolley I lay upon moved on further. I heard a curtain open and close.

"This one's weird," a woman said.

"You can say that again. We'll get her changed into a gown and then take her blood to run some tests."

I felt everything, but I couldn't do anything. My body was stripped bare. The coolness in the room swept over my skin, then something was placed over me. My arms were pulled through and I was pushed to the side where I felt someone's fingers at my back doing up ties. I hated hospital gowns. They were uncomfortable and still flashed things no one should see. I was thankful they'd left my underwear on; however, they'd taken my bra, so the girls were swinging free. A blanket was thrown over me and next, a needle was jabbed into my arm, I cursed through the feel of blood being drawn from my body.

"Did you see her man out the front?"

"No, is he nice?"

"He's hot, but it's taking the two men with him to keep him out there. Poor guy wants to see his woman."

"Why don't they let him in?"

"They're worried he'll just get in the way with the way he's acting..."

"Damn. Okay, go run those through. We need answers now—who are you?"

"You don't need to worry about that."

Oh, shit.

Oh, damn.

Fuck.

It was Oscar.

"Both of you back the fuck off her. I need to take her."

"You can't do that. We need to find out what's wrong with her."

Oscar chuckled. "Easy, I had someone put a homemade roofy in her teabags, one where it numbs the whole body, but the little bitch is still awake on the inside. Isn't that right, you fucking whore." I felt his hand on my face, running over my lips and down my cheek. "We're going to have a blast together." He laughed.

"Y-you need to stay away from her," the one who had taken my blood said.

"Afraid I can't do that."

Movement spun around me and then two gasps sounded.

"Back the fuck off or I'll shoot you both. I'm taking her."

No, no, he can't do this. Move, you stupid body, move, scream, fight.

"Don't be silly and budge from that spot," he ordered. The blanket that covered me was thrown from my body.

God, no, please, no. Yell for Declan. Yell for help. Please, help me. Don't let him take me. Get my man. My man will save me.

An arm was forced under my neck and another, which held cold metal—the gun?—was slid under my legs. I was picked up from the bed.

"Get back. Jesus, fuck, you can't go out there and say anything." He placed my useless body back on the bed and I heard him walk away.

"No, we won't say anything. We'll stay in this room."

Oscar snorted. "Yeah, right."

"No," one screamed. Then there was a thump, something crashed to the floor.

"Don't please," a nurse begged. There was a scuffle, slaps, grunts, another thump and something else fell to the floor.

"Now you won't say anything." He chuckled.

Oh, my God, what had he done to them?

"Fucking stop the tears. They'll be fine. I only kill stupid bitches like you," Oscar said, again he lifted me from the bed. "Jesus, even when you're like this, you annoy me. The world will be better off without you in it... after you've told me what you know and I've had some fun with your body."

My stomach churned. Not only from his words, but from the touch of his skin on my bare legs and neck.

"Coast is clear, lucky you," he mocked and started to walk out of the room, and from the sound of his shoes on vinyl flooring, down a hall.

"Hey... w-what are you doing?"

"Fuck," Oscar hissed. He turned and said with confidence, "I was told to take this patient to another room."

"We have wheelchairs for that and she should have already been on a bed that could also wheel her."

"Whoops, didn't think of that."

"Are you new here?"

"Sure am. First day on the job. Look, she's getting heavy. I need to keep going."

With all my strength and mind, I forced my arm to move. *Fuck!* I managed an inch of movement and that was it.

Oh, God.

Would I ever see my kids again?

Declan?

Tears ran down my face.

"Is she okay?"

"Look, dickhead, does she look okay?" With that, I felt Oscar turn once again and start forward. The doctor or nurse, whoever that guy was said nothing more.

Dooming me to my fate.

STOKE

The waiting was killing me and I was sure my brothers had enough of fighting me back to a seat after I tried to run for the goddamn doors again, and again.

"Don't make me sit on you, fucker," Dodge hissed. He was seated beside me instead of Blue, who I accidentally gave a bloody nose to when I elbowed him in the face, fighting my way into the hospital.

Stupid. I was being stupid, overreacting.

But fuck, until I saw Malinda, until I knew she was okay, I was living on the edge of releasing my demon inside. It wanted to claw its way out and hurt anything and everything that was keeping me from my woman.

"Fuck, brother, remind me never to get a woman if this is how crazy we act," Dodge complained.

"I can't wait for your turn, dickhead," Killer said from the other side of me.

"Ain't happening if you turn into a pussy like this." Dodge laughed.

Turning, I grabbed him by his tee and threw him to the ground. Sneering down at him, I demanded, "Is it being a pussy when you see someone you love drop to the ground and you don't know why? You see tears fall from your woman's eyes while her body is still, not moving in your arms and you can't do anything about it. If that's being a pussy, then I don't give a fuck."

"Learn to shut the fuck up, Dodge," Killer said.

"Shit, yeah, all right. I get it. Don't kill me, man."

Their talking was pissing me off. I knew they were doing it for my benefit but it didn't help.

Shit. Nothing would help until I had my woman.

My eyes were to the ground. I was leaning forward, ready to bolt, or throw up. I leaned on my knees that bounced up and down, from my feet on the vinyl floor and my sweaty hands were clasped tightly together in front of me.

Tilting my head to the side as heavy pounding footsteps caught my attention, my cousin came running around a corner.

"Let him go," Lan yelled.

I bounced up to my feet, ready to take anything on.

Killer grabbed one arm, Dodge the other. But it was Killer who said, "Fuckin' hell, Stoke, get a grip. You ain't doing Malinda any favours acting like this."

Closing my eyes, I took a deep breath.

He was right. I knew it, but logic wasn't my friend right then.

"No," Lan barked, still yelling words that sliced a knife right through my heart. "Let him the fuck in there. Go, Stoke, find your woman. Oscar is here somewhere."

"Fuck!" I roared and ran for the emergency doors. Security men tried to get in my way, but I barrelled through them. The doors hit the walls as I pushed them wide.

"Malinda?" I screamed.

"Sir, you can't be in here," a nurse said.

"Woman, I'd advise you to give us his woman's room and now," Dodge ordered.

Lan came through behind us. "We need Malinda May's

room now. We have reason to believe a criminal is in there with her."

"That's ridiculous," an older woman laughed.

I turned to her and skewered her with my gaze. "Fuckin' tell me now," I yelled.

She paled and uttered, "Down the hall to the left, room 205."

I ran for it, my brothers and cousin at my back. Everyone got out of the way, some screamed, some gasped, hell, some even cursed. They all looked scared, but I didn't care.

I gripped the curtain, and with my strength, instead of pulling it aside, I pulled it from its rails and it drifted to the floor. I stepped in and yelled, "Motherfucker." Two nurses were knocked out on the floor, bruises already showed on their foreheads.

"Dodge, stay here with them," Talon ordered. Where he came from, I didn't have a fucking clue. I turned and started running again.

What caught my attention was a male nurse shakily raise his hand, and with a finger, he pointed toward a hallway. When I turned, I saw at the end a Goddamn motherfucking exit sign.

Pulling my gun from the back of my jeans, I strode down it.

"Let me go first," Lan said.

"No,"

"Cousin,"

"No," I barked.

"Let him do this. He needs to do this," Killer said.

"Fuck, I'm a cop. I should be the one. He can get into shit over this."

"Can he?" Talon asked. "As far as I see, you're the only cop here."

"You can't ask this of me."

"Enough," I snapped and pushed the exit door open.

My eyes searched the area. It was a huge-arse loading dock with trucks and shit everywhere.

"There," Talon pointed.

Just beyond a truck, I spotted a car, only the back of it was visible. When I saw it, my blood boiled and then pumped faster through my veins. "Oscar," I rumbled low as Talon sent out orders. I didn't listen. I started down the steps and headed straight for the man who was about to die.

He had Malinda's limp form in his arms as he struggled to open the back door.

"Oscar," I roared.

He spun, nearly dropping Malinda to the concrete ground. "Back the fuck up or I'll kill her." He slid her from his arms and sat her propped up against the car in seconds. The movement would have hurt her if she had been awake. Oscar then took aim at me. I didn't flinch. I didn't think. I just kept my fast pace toward him.

"Stop," he yelled.

"You dare take my woman? You dare take her from here and harm her? You say nothing and do nothing more. You hear me, fucker?"

"I. Will. Kill. Her! Even before you get to me." He switched the gun from me and pointed it at my woman's head.

My body locked. I stood frozen. "Leave her and you won't be harmed. Leave her and stay the fuck away."

He snorted. "I'm not fuckin' stupid."

Looking over Oscar, I smirked and said, "No, you're wrong. You're stupid, to think I'd be out here on my own."

A shot was fired. Oscar went to his knees. He raised his gun to me with wide panicked eyes and fired. I dove to the left, my body landing hard.

Killer showed up beside me as I tried to sit up. "Don't fuckin' move. You've been hit. I need help here. Stoke's down," he yelled.

Not a-fucking-gain. Christ.

"Malinda?" I asked.

"She's fine. Talon's taking her inside."

"Good." I grinned, then like a girly man, I passed the fuck out.

EPILOGUE

ONE MONTH LATER

STOKE

I was lying awake in bed with my woman at my side. My mind was busy thinking of the time I nearly lost her. I woke every morning thinking she'd been taken from me, and it fucking hurt. It took me sometime to calm my heart and realise my woman lay at my side. Her head always up against my arm or on my chest. Her arm always flung over my stomach.

Fuck. I hated and loved how I woke. I hated it because it put fright into my body and mind. I loved it when the fog in my brain cleared and I felt her against me.

When I woke after my operation to remove the bullet

from my shoulder, I opened my eyes and saw my woman standing at the end of my bed with her hands on her hips, scowling down at me. Christ, she looked beautiful, even in the simplicity of jeans and a cashmere jumper. Her hair was down around her shoulders. Her eyes were glaring at me, but they shined the gorgeous green just for me. I smiled; she growled.

"Next time you save me—though, I really hope there won't be a next time—you *will not* risk your life in doing so. It was a jerk move, no matter what you were going through." Her breath hitched; tears filled her eyes. "If... if anything were to happen to you... I couldn't recover from it, Declan Stoke." She swiped her tears away. "Never do that to me again. I love you too much, so much it scares me."

"Come here, love."

"No, I'm still angry with you."

"Malinda, come here."

She bit her bottom lip to stop it quivering.

"Love, please. You scared me, too. I need to feel my woman."

She sighed and walked to the side of the bed. When she was close, I reached out, tagged her hand and pulled her onto the bed with me. Thank fuck, she chose to the side my good arm was.

She tried to scramble off, but I wrapped my arm around her waist and tugged her down to my side.

"I'll hurt you."

"Fuck, no, you won't," I growled and planted my nose into her hair, taking a deep breath. "I thought I'd lost you. It killed me, love. Killed me." Nipping her neck, I added, "You're mine."

"Yes," she sighed contently.

"We're gonna get hitched and I'm gonna fill your belly with my seed. I want more kids with you, love. I want one of our blood, even though I see Josh and Nary as mine already. I want more. I'm moving in, selling my house and putting a ring on your finger. And there ain't shit you can do about it."

She harrumphed. "Well, I guess it's good I agree then."

I chuckled. "Yeah, it is."

She got up to her elbow and looked down at me. "You see them as your kids?"

"Yeah."

"I love you, Deck." She smiled with new tears in her eyes.

"Love, you were made for me and so were your kids. I fuckin' love you all."

"Good, but don't think you're getting out of a good talking to about what you did."

Jesus.

That was when I found out my woman had been awake on the inside. She heard everything and was petrified outta her mind. Not for her safety, for mine. She went on to explain the kids had their own kind of shit go down at Beth's house. Which explained why moments later, I got a new goddamn roommate, Mrs fucking Cliff was wheeled in, her bed parked next to mine.

The week in hospital had me seriously contemplating suicide.

The whole day was busy with visitors, nurses and

doctors. I didn't get a chance to find out until later, when Mrs Cliff was asleep and I rang Killer, what happened with Oscar.

Lan had been the one to shoot him in the leg. As Talon took Malinda inside and Killer stuck with me, Lan and Dodge loaded up Oscar into that car and took off.

Apparently, they had left me a surprise for when I got out and I couldn't wait to delivery payback before we handed him over to Anthony. What surprised the shit outta me was that Lan was allowing it.

Which meant... shit, I was grateful and prepared to let him in my life more, even if he had a thing for my woman.

Killer also said that Malcolm was still in a holding cell at the compound. Beth had told me in more detail all about Malcolm's little visit. The little shit wanted to take my girl again. He deserved what he got, so I told Killer to let Saxon do with him what he wanted, but then he had to hand him over to Lan. At least Lan would then get something; seemed the little mongrel was in cahoots with Oscar.

A week later, once released, I went to the compound and got to see Saxon's handy work, and hell, it made me proud of the bugger. Lan was leading Malcolm out. After sending my cousin a chin lift, I looked to Malcolm to see he had a split lip. At least five fingers were broken, plus his face was swollen and he was limping as Lan dragged him down the hallway.

"Have fun in jail, dickhead," I sang. I hoped he'd get his arse virginity taken by some huge motherfucker.

I kept walking and opened the next door. I took in what greeted me in the small concrete room. Killer, Dodge, Dive, and Talon were standing around, and in the middle of the room sat Oscar on an old kitchen chair.

"'Bout time you got here," Dodge said.

"Shut-up, fucker. I had to heal."

"You're still an ugly shit. I thought you were getting a facelift."

I snorted out laughter. Dodge the fuckin' wanker.

"Let's get this done. Anthony wants him this afternoon," Talon ordered.

"My pleasure." I smiled.

Oscar glared up at me, silent the whole time until I moved toward him. "I'll get away and I'll find your whore and cut her so bad you won't want to fuck her."

"Oh, Jesus," Dive whistled. "We may need a doc in here after Stoke's done with him, before he goes to Anthony."

Killer scoffed. "That's probably what he wants, to die before Anthony gets him."

Shaking my head, I said, "Ain't gonna work because I know sooner or later, you'll be a dead man." I held out my hand and Killer deposited a knife in it.

Oscar, with his hands tied behind his back, started to scoot his chair away from me. I sent a chin lift to Dive and Dodge. They walked to him and stood him up.

He struggled from them and cried, "Don't, fuck, please don't. I won't go after her. She'll be safe, please."

"Too late." I grinned. Killer went behind him and took down his pants.

"Wait, wait! What are you doing?"

Hitting the knife against my palm, I explained, "You see, my woman told me what you and you little mate had planned for her and Nary. You wanted to fuck her and then use a knife to fuck her. So I thought I'd give it a try on you."

Not that I did. I ain't a sick fucker.

But apparently, from what I did do, you could hear his screams all over the compound.

MY WOMAN STIRRED in the bed beside me. Her arm over my stomach tightened, her leg coming up mine before slowly going back down.

How was I so fucking lucky to have such a beauty in bed with me? A woman who loved with her whole heart and would share and shine on you if, in return, you loved and cherished her. Which I did, deep in my bones, blood and soul. I fucking cherished the ground she walked on, and in a goddamn moment, I was gonna cherish her body if she didn't quit with the little wake-up sounds.

Her arms came up outta the blanket as she lay on her back and stretched. A moan fell from her lips, and even though I'd had her the previous night, I needed her again.

I went to my side and winced as the lingering pain in my shoulder hit me. Still, I ignored it and rolled further so half of my body went over hers. She blinked her eyes open and smiled.

"Morning, handsome."

"Mornin', love," I growled. "You know, it should be illegal the way my cock wants to live in your pussy."

She threw her head back into the pillow even more and burst out laughing. I grinned. I fucking loved seeing her laugh; she put all effort into it and laughed with her whole body.

After she settled down, I asked, "Your pussy up for some punishing?"

Her lips twitched. "Depends, what's it being punished for?"

"For being too fuckin' perfect."

She snorted. "You're an idiot." She grinned, reached down and wound her hand around my hard cock, ripping a groan outta me.

"I'm an idiot for you," I said and touched my tongue to her neck, licking all the way up to her ear, where I bit down on her lobe. I slid my hand into her panties. Panties she must have put on through the night. Eagerly, she spread her legs for me; Christ, she was already soaked. I ran my finger up and down her pussy lips.

"Oh, God, please idiot away on me," she moaned.

"I will, love," I whispered and then stole her lips for a kiss. She opened her mouth for me straight away. Slipping my tongue in, I slid two fingers inside of her tight snatch. Her hips came off the bed as her hand wanking my cock tightened.

"Fuck, woman,"

"Yes, fuck me," she said and kissed me again.

I pulled my hand out of her and ripped her panties down. I moved her to her side, lifted her leg and slid home. She moaned loudly as I grunted and shoved my face in her hair. Slowly and deeply, I fucked my woman's pussy, driving in and out with ease because she was so wet.

Letting go of her leg, I reached around and grabbed her

breast, tweaking her nipples and massaging her breasts. She loved tit action. One day I'd get to fuck 'em. I just knew it.

"Deck, yes! God, I'm going to come."

"Hold it, love. Fuck, hold it. We'll come together," I ordered.

Sweat beaded over our bodies, our breaths panted out together as I drilled my cock into my woman's pussy.

"Now," I growled and as soon as I did, her walls clamped around my dick and she cried out my name in pleasure. "Yes," I hissed and pumped my seed into her welcoming pussy.

AFTER WE'D MANAGED to get out of bed, I left Malinda in the shower and made my way into the kitchen where I found Josh and Nary.

"Thought you two were at Beth's?" I no longer called Beth, Mrs Cliff. Since staying in the same room at the fuckin' hospital, I started calling her by her name. She told me it was disrespectful, so, of course, I kept at it. There was no way in hell I was gonna go back now.

"We did, quickly did our jobs cleaning her place, but left as soon as we could. She's worse when she's in a foul mood," Josh said.

Her gunshot wound, similar to mine in the shoulder, was still acting up. She couldn't do what she usually would and made her one-hundred times worse than what she usually was.

"Was Dallas there?" I asked as I grabbed two coffee mugs.

"No, he bailed as soon as we walked through the door," Nary complained. Dallas had decided to stay in town and get outta the Army. He was actually thinking of joining Hawks. Talon was more than happy to have him patched in. He was a good man, though, quiet.

The back door banged open. "Fuck this," Griz growled as he stalked in... holding a German Shepard puppy.

"Brother, what's up?" I smirked.

"My wife bought that witch next door this mutt. She don't want it. She said if this thing stayed in her house, then she'd be moving in with us. I said over my fuckin' dead, shrivelled body. She said that could be arranged." He went over to Nary, placed the dog in her arms and said, 'Here, you guys keep it."

"Now, hang the fuck on. You can't just come in here and give my kids a goddamn puppy. I ain't cleaning up its shit and piss. We ain't havin' a dog."

Griz ignored me and said, "By the way, my woman's little fluff ball of a stupid dog, dug up Beth's backyard, another reason she didn't want a dog, but guess what it found?"

"What?"

"Let's just say Anthony Graham won't be giving you any trouble."

"Shit, seriously."

"Yeah." He grinned.

That was a huge relief.

I heard a sniffle and looked to Nary. She had tears pouring outta her. My head went back, my eyes widened and I asked, "What you cryin' for?"

"Nothing," she whispered.

"Bullshit," I said. Fuck, if she wanted the dog that badly, she could have it. I didn't want to see my girl crying over it.

"Can we call you dad now?" Josh asked.

My head spun to him, my heart thumped hard in my chest. "What?"

"You called us *your* kids. That's why she's crying like a girl. So can we call you dad now?" he explained.

Well, shit.

A sob tore through the kitchen. I looked to see Malinda standing in the doorway. Tears ran down her face, ruining her makeup. "Yes," she said. "You can call him dad and we're keeping the cute puppy."

"You're fucked, brother," Griz chuckled.

I was, because my woman was gonna get her way. Not that I was stressing over it. I felt goddam privileged the kids wanted to call me dad. The thing that worried me, that Griz saw, was that the situation showed me how things were gonna be for the future—the women of the house getting their way—but hell, I didn't care at all.

I was happy.

SNEAK PEEK — COMING OUT

HAWKS MC: BALLARAT CHARTER #4.5

CHAPTER ONE

MATTIE

A year before reuniting with Zara.

The locker room was rowdy and cold. It didn't help I was staring blindly into my locker wearing only a towel. Droplets of water cascaded down my body, dripping onto the floor. A shiver raked through me responding to the frigid air. Damn, had Coach even turned on the heat? I didn't know. I knew nothing but the thoughts destroying my brain. I was a fake, an idiot, and more significantly, scared. For four years, I'd pretended to be someone I wasn't. Four years of hiding who I was from my family; four years of hurting others in my life because I was weak.

"Hey, Alexander," Peterson called, poking his head

around the corner of the lockers. "Coach got a masseur and it's your turn. But watch your arse. You can just tell the guy's gay."

Once he disappeared, I banged my head against my locker.

Could Peterson, or any of the guys on the football team tell I was gay?

No.

Because I made sure no one knew.

Why?

Because I was a phoney.

I made sure they saw me with random women, drinking and, even worse, talking shit about gay people. Each time, every comment made me sick to the stomach.

But I knew how they were. They hated people like me. They picked on and taunted people like me.

However, what caused me to shut my mouth for so long, what caused me to keep to myself about liking men, was what happened three years earlier. Witnessing some meat-heads bash a guy for being gay, punching out their disgust with every hit and kick, sealed my decision to live a lie.

Bang. My head made contact with the locker.

Shit. Why am I so weak?

It wasn't like my parents wouldn't understand and support me no matter what. Heck, I knew they'd love me if I wanted to be the next Madonna in drag. Even my alpha ex-army dad, would tell me I was being stupid pretending to be someone I wasn't.

Some days, I wished my sister was still around to talk to,

to confide in. But she wasn't and she couldn't be there because of yet another meat-head jerk.

Still, a small amount of worry constantly seeped in, especially worry that my sister would turn me away—she'd hate that I was gay. Though, she did have a huge heart, so I could only hope she wouldn't. I was being selfish for wanting her there. I was being selfish for wanting to load my troubles onto her when she had her own crap to deal with, and her crap was a lot worse than mine. Zara, my twenty-five-year-old sister, was on the run for her life, to save not only herself, but her daughter from the man she married when she was my age, nineteen.

So she needed to stay safe, which was also why I didn't ring or Skype with her. She'd be able to tell something was wrong and she'd come home, so I couldn't chance it. No matter how much I needed or wanted her support.

Hell, I had to man up and soon, for my own sanity. Which was why, later that night, I was heading home to tell my parents I was gay.

It was a start at least, even if it scared me. I was sick of being weak.

"Alexander." Coach boomed my name.

"Coming," I yelled.

"Not bloody fast enough," Coach grumbled as I walked around the corner. "Good, you're still in your towel," he said, eyeing me up and down quickly. "It's your turn to take a rub-down. New system the sponsors are doin' for their players on the university team, to keep you all playing and happy." He snorted. "We'll see how long that lasts."

"Hmm." There seemed little else for me to say. It was

easy to pretend the reason why I chose to play football was for my love of it and the experience. In reality, I knew better. It was a good front with the meat-head idiots.

I shrugged. The pretence wouldn't matter soon enough anyway, because I was going to quit. I planned to leave the team as soon as I came out of the closet. It'd save all the shit that'd be, no doubt, flung my way.

Opening the door a few rooms down from Coach's office, I walked in with my head hanging low. My mind was occupied on other things, until I heard, "Lie on the table, face down." My head snapped up to the owner of the sad voice and my eyes landed on the most handsome man I had ever seen. He was tall. My head tilted a little to look up at him and then my eyes drifted down to see his upper arms showing he held muscle, enough to make me want to see what was under his white tee. His hair was darker than my brown, short and unruly hair. His moss green eyes glared at me.

Shit. My dick behind the flimsy towel twitched.

"Come on, I don't have all day."

How many men had he touched already? How many men did he still have to touch?

Thinking about it pissed me off. My nostrils flared, my body flushed in anger and I found myself clenching my jaw.

I wanted to be the only one who he had his hands on. I wanted to…yeah, I *wanted* him. A shudder ran through my body imagining his hands on me. I couldn't wait, the sooner the better, especially if my dick continued to grow hard.

A snort touched my ears. I looked to his face as I approached the table. His nose twitched, his eyes were hard, like he was angry at me. Also within his eyes, I saw they held a certain amount of hurt.

I could only assume he mistook the shudder for disgust or annoyance when I felt the exact opposite. I was turned on and the locker room was the worst place to be aroused.

"I..." I started, only I didn't know what to say. I couldn't say anything. Instead, I flattened my sore body onto the table. My face rested in the hole at the end, immediately making me think of slipping into another hole.

Jesus. I needed to get laid. My thoughts were going to get me in trouble.

When his hands touched my skin, I jumped, and as soon as his warm hands bit into my muscles, I clamped my top teeth down on my bottom lip to keep from moaning.

I needed to say something, anything.

"You..."

Fuck it. That was obviously the best I could do.

"Yes, I'm gay, but don't worry your pretty little head over it. You don't do anything for me." While his voice contained anger, it sounded deflated.

Wait.

He thought I was pretty?

Handsome I could stand.

But pretty?

Wait.

He also said I didn't do anything for him.

Damn.

"I-I don't care." I clenched my hands as his magical fingers worked my back. Would it be ridiculous if I purred?

Christ, I sounded like my sister. She always thought and voiced strange stuff.

The man snorted and dug in his hands harder into my lower back.

Goddamn, go lower. LOWER.

"What—you don't care that you don't do anything for me, or that I'm gay?"

Great. If I said yes to both then he'd know I was... inclined his way. If I said yes to the last, then he wouldn't suspect. Something told me I wanted to wait and shock him on a later date. The game would be fun. It'd also give me a chance to get to know him.

"The last," I answered. "What's your name?"

"Julian. Why you asking, sugar? You want to scream my name later when you're fisting your cock?"

My eyes widened at the thought, a thought that sounded mighty fine.

Instead, I scoffed. "No."

He hummed to himself. I would have loved to have known what he was thinking. "What's your name?" he asked.

"Matthew," I said as he worked my back. Was he going to go low or not?

My question was answered moments later when his hands suddenly left me and landed on my upper thighs. He squeezed them. I closed my eyes and mouthed, *Fuck.*

"Do you like my hands on you, Mattie?" he drawled, running his hands slowly up and down the back of my legs, just inches shy of my lower arse cheeks.

Please keep going, my dick sang.

What am I doing? my mind thought.

But shit, I knew it was a test, either that or he was looking to get fired on his first day.

So I played his game. "Sure, you're good at what you do."

He growled low. I smirked.

"The other guys were running from the room by now," he said.

Shrugging, I said, "Why do you want to get fired?"

He stopped, his hands fell away, and I turned to see his surprised face. Surprised I had figured him out maybe.

Shit, he was so good-looking. I wanted to do so many things to him. I wanted to roll over and show him my erection to see his reaction. I wanted to run my hands over him, like he had me, only I would have taken it further.

However, I did none of those. I couldn't and it annoyed me, pissed me off. I sat up from the table, my back to him and I secured the towel firmly around my waist. I glanced over my shoulder and said, "Why don't you just leave?"

I knew it sounded harsh and I knew he'd take it the wrong way. I meant why did he want to get fired? Why couldn't he just leave if he didn't like the job? Still, I didn't correct my mistake, even when I saw the pain in his eyes, and the flinch in his body when he *did* take my words the wrong way. I did nothing but stand and walk out of the room, leaving me feeling like a prick.

I knew Julian would be plaguing my mind from that day out.

After I showered to get the oils from my skin, I dressed and made my way home. It was hard—pun intended—not to masturbate in the shower, thinking of Julian and his hands, but there were teammates around still.

I did think of staying until they all left. Mainly because I was worried that if Julian played the same game with all of my team mates, he could get hurt, and I didn't like the thought.

However, because I knew Coach was working late, I figured he also wouldn't let anything happen, so I left.

On the way home though was another story. My mind plagued me and I'd ended up turning my car around to check he was okay. I did this so many times, only to turn it back around and head for home. Somehow, after many inner arguments, I still ended up pulling into my driveway, technically my parents' driveway, because I still lived with them. That was until I found the perfect place for myself. I'd saved and was still saving enough money with my casual job at the local real estate office that I hoped I would soon find the right house to move to.

After I dropped the 'gay' bomb, I would need my own place so much more. My mum could be...a lot to handle sometimes, always questioning when I would settle down, when I would bring home the 'right' girls instead of the sluts I was shagging. *Her words, not mine.*

Stepping into the cool night air pulled a shiver from me. I shouldered my backpack and made my way to the front door when it opened. I found a smiling Mum standing in the doorway.

"Let me guess, you were just skyping Zara?" I asked as I kissed her cheek, and slipped in past her.

Mum clapped her hands and gleefully said, "Yes, and I saw Maya. She is such a cutie. Then I spoke with Deanna. That woman sure can cuss like a sailor."

"How is everybody?" I moved my backpack to the floor near the front door and followed Mum into the kitchen where Dad was at the kitchen sink carving the roast meat. Looked like lamb.

"Don't forget to take your bag to your room before I fall over it," she said before adding, "They're all doing great. We talked about going to Melbourne one day to meet with them. Isn't that wonderful? We just need to sort a few things out—"

"Like what?" I laughed. "You're both retired." Mum was a retired nurse and Dad was an ex-army man.

Dad put the knife down and said, "Son, you know I have bowls, darts, and other shit to do. I can't just up and leave them. People would be lost without me. Then there's also all the crap your mother does."

"Crap?" Mum demanded with her hands on her hips. "Do you even know what I do these days, Rich?"

Dad rolled his eyes at Mum's dramatics. I made myself busy setting the table while they bickered to each other.

"Yes, Nancy. I know everything you do and all of it is amazing, great, super and fantastic."

"Don't patronise me or you'll be sleeping on the couch," Mum snapped as she placed the vegetables on the kitchen table.

"Drink?" I asked.

"Thank you, sweetie, I'll have a glass of wine," Mum said and then slapped Dad's hand away from the meat he was stealing.

"I carved it, woman. Beer me, boy," Dad said gruffly, then walked around the counter and placed the tray of meat on the table.

Their relationship was…strange, but full of love. I often wondered if I would ever get to have something that precious in my life. I wanted to meet my other half, the one who would put up with my shit, like Mum does with Dad, or vice-versa.

Julian.

Laughing at my own thought, I sat down at the table. I looked to my Dad who took a swig of his beer, and I blurted, "I'm gay."

Of course, he spat his beer all over the table, his wide eyes meeting mine as the rest dribbled down his chin. He took the back of his hand up to wipe it away. I couldn't look at Mum. For some reason, I needed to hear, to see, what Dad thought or said first.

My heart beat out of my chest. My palms, lying on my thighs, sweated. I wanted to jump out of my own body, find those words I just said and shove them down my throat again. The silence was killing me.

Then he shrugged and took another sip of his beer before he said, "Don't bother me, son. As long as you're happy with what you are, with who you want to be with, it ain't got shit to do with me. I just want you happy, kid. If you like cock more than—"

"Richard," Mum yelled.

Dad chuckled. "It don't make a difference to me, Matthew. I love ya no matter."

My eyes stung. I clenched my jaw tightly together and sniffed. Shit. I never...why had I been so scared to tell them? I didn't know. I was stupid, that was the reason why.

Turning my watery eyes to Mum, I saw she was just as bad as me; her emotions were running the show. Her bottom lip trembled and then she smiled, rose from her seat, and I scooted back as she advanced on me, her hands going to my cheeks. "You're a brave, smart, handsome man. Nothing will change how much we love you."

"Mum," I choked.

She shushed me, kissed my forehead and pulled back to stand, that was when she said, "Now, do you have a special someone you can introduce us to?"

Blushing, I thought of Julian once again. When she was seated, I answered, "No...not yet."

"Okay, well, when the time comes, we'll want to meet him. Need to make sure he'll be good enough for our boy."

Jeesh. That was something I wasn't looking forward to. Mum would no doubt embarrass me by asking inappropriate things.

For example, the next words out of her mouth, "Do you take or give?"

"Nancy," Dad barked. "Jesus Christ, woman."

Mum rolled her eyes. "I'm just curious."

"Mum, it's not something to discuss at dinner...or ever."

She sighed. "Fine. Now get some grub into you."

SNEAK PEEK — THE SECRET'S OUT

HAWKS MC: CAROLINE SPRINGS
CHARTER: BOOK 1

TWO YEARS LATER

Nancy Alexandra placed her phone on the table. She looked down, but wasn't really focused on it. No, her mind was running over things from the phone call she just had.

Her youngest daughter, Josie, hadn't been home that Christmas holidays. In fact, she hadn't returned home in a long time and Nancy was worried. For the tenth time that day, she called her daughter's mobile demanding answers. Only it wasn't her daughter who supplied them.

Josie's roommate, where she lived in a small apartment close to her school, had answered.

"Mrs Alexandra?" she whispered into the phone. Nancy should have realised then that something was wrong, but she didn't.

"Simone, honey, how many times do I have to tell you to call me Nancy? Now, can you tell me where my daughter is?

I'm getting sick of this run around. She's either too busy to talk or on her way out somewhere. I'm worried about my girl, Simone."

"You should be," Simone uttered and Nancy started to panic.

Nancy sat straight in her chair. "Tell me, Simone."

"It's not really my place."

"No, Simone, you tell me now so I can help."

"She won't want her mum here. That'll make things worse."

"Simone. Tell. Me!"

"Josie's in the bathroom, I can hear her crying. She cries a lot, Nancy, and I think it has to do with some guys who are hassling her. She's so quiet and timid; the stupid-heads find it fun to cause her problems."

"Is that all?" Nancy snapped in a hard tone.

"I- I think so? Please, please don't come here. I swear it'll make things worse."

"Oh, I won't come, darling. I'll be sending someone else."

"Who?"

"Doesn't matter. Just know help will be arriving soon, watch over my girl 'til then."

"I will, Mrs—I mean, Nancy."

"Thank you, Simone, for telling me."

"I hate seeing Josie upset."

"I do also. I'm going to let you go now. I need to make a phone call."

Simone hung up the phone and not long after, Nancy stared at the phone on the table thinking. She picked it back up again and put it to her ear.

"Hello, my wonderful son-in-law."

"Nancy," was all Talon said.

"Josie is having trouble as school. Some guys are… annoying her, Talon." Usually Nancy would taunt him to get a rise, but she wasn't in the mood, and her son-in-law knew it by her tone.

"Fuck," Talon growled low. "I'll handle it."

"Good," Nancy said and hung up.

ACKNOWLEDGEMENTS

To my Lila Muffkateer group, you have all helped me so much, not only with the title of this book, but for Stoke's first name. I really appreciate all your help and support. Thank you. (Malinda, thanks for letting me steal your name)

Neringa, thank you for being such a wonderful, thoughtful person.

Lindsey Lawson, you, like many, have been here from the start. I appreciate everything you do and thank the high Heaven you entered my very first giveaway because it wouldn't be the same without your friendship.

Becky at Hot Tree Editing, working with you is always a pleasure. If it wasn't for your wise advice, I honestly doubt my work would be any good. And thanks to Sue, Debbie and Jill for your beta reading skills.

Josie and Becky at Hot Tree Promotions, thank you for all you do. You work so hard and I am thankful for it every time!

Justine Littleton, people must be getting sick of seeing your name in my acknowledgments, but I have to thank you every time. Not only are you a great, amazing friend, but you're also my brain. I love having you to run things by. Thanks for always being there!

Rachel Morgan, you are the perfect sister. Not only do I have your love and support, but you also give me the best friendship I have ever had.

Mum, thank you for your constant support, for reading my work, even if sometimes it drives you to seek therapy. Love you, Ma!

Christine, Harry, Mathew, Christopher and Jessica, thank you for all your encouragement.

Robyn, Wyatt, and my annoying brother, Darren, thanks for believing in me.

Always, a huge thank you to my husband, Craig (tool man) my daughter Shayla, and my son Jake.

Romantic comedies

Making Changes

Making Sense

Fumbled Love

Trinity Love Series

Left to Chance

Love of Liberty (novella)

Paranormal

Death (with Justine Littleton)

In The Dark

CONNECT WITH LILA ROSE

Webpage: www.lilarosebooks.com

Facebook: http://bit.ly/2du0taO

Instagram: www.instagram.com/lilarose78/

Goodreads:

www.goodreads.com/author/show/7236200.Lila_Rose

Printed in the USA
CPSIA information can be obtained
at www.ICGtesting.com
LVHW020828271123
764961LV00015B/833